CODE WORD COURAGE

ALSO BY KIRBY LARSON

Novels

Audacity Jones to the Rescue

Audacity Jones Steals the Show

Duke

Dash

Liberty

Dear America: *The Fences Between Us*

The Friendship Doll

Hattie Big Sky

Hattie Ever After

Picture Books
with Mary Nethery

Nubs: The True Story of a Mutt, a Marine & a Miracle

Two Bobbies: A True Story of Hurricane Katrina, Friendship, and Survival

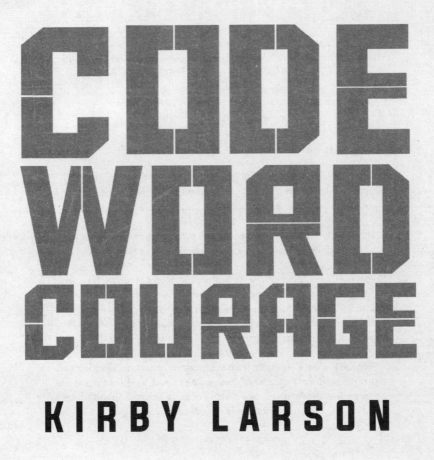

CODE WORD COURAGE

KIRBY LARSON

SCHOLASTIC INC.

Copyright © 2018 by Kirby Larson

This book was originally published in hardcover by Scholastic Press in 2018.

ISBN 978-0-545-84076-7

10 9 8 7 6 5 4 3 2 1   19 20 21 22 23

Printed in the U.S.A.   40
This edition first printing January 2019

Book design by Maeve Norton

For the Code Talkers—
Ahé hee' for your service

TABLE OF CONTENTS

The dog did not want to leave the vehicle. Did not want to follow the man. But the rope prevented any other option.

"Pa!" a voice cried from the backseat. "Pa! Don't. Please don't!"

The dog whined to hear his boy so upset. As soon as the man loosened the rope from his neck, he scrambled to return to the car.

The man raised his arm. Hollered. "Git." He pelted the dog with rocks scooped up from the highway shoulder.

Too many of the sharp edges found their marks. And then a large stone cracked something in his side. Try as he might, the dog could no longer stand his ground. Panting to ease the pain, he limped out of range.

A door slammed, then the vehicle sped down the highway. The dog struggled to follow. But his legs gave way and he collapsed in the dirt. He didn't try to get up again.

Without his boy, there was no point.

PART ONE

"Many people will walk in and out of your life, but only true friends will leave footprints in your heart."

—Eleanor Roosevelt

CHAPTER ONE

Billie

Friday, September 22, 1944

Billie Packer didn't need to be a detective to figure out who'd shot the spit wad now glued to her pigtail. Not from the way Spinner Greeley and Del Randall were yukking it up a few seats back.

Doff said such attentions were a boy's way of saying he liked a girl. But Doff was somewhere north of seventy years old, and didn't realize that, in 1944, most boys did not shoot spit wads as a sign of affection. Nor did they steal milk money or accidentally-on-purpose trip people.

Billie pulled her hair away from her face, trying to summon the courage to touch the disgusting thing stuck there. This was more than a potential case of boy cooties. Spinner and Del suffered from a fatal case of the stupids, a disease she definitely didn't want to catch.

The new kid reached across the bus aisle. "Here," he said.

She hesitated. What kind of fifth grader carried handkerchiefs? "It's all ironed and everything," she protested.

"Mamá would iron *me* if I stood still long enough." His smile lit up brown eyes behind a pair of horn-rimmed glasses. "Go on. Take it."

"Thanks." They were practically neighbors, but this was the first time they'd spoken. "Tito."

Spinner shot another spit wad, which bounced off the back of Billie's seat. Kit McDonald giggled. "Nice shot!" she said. Hazel French joined the laughter.

Billie squinched her eyes in her former best pal's direction. Right about the time Leo left for boot camp, Hazel had fallen under Kit's spell and her brain had been turned to mush over boys and movie stars. And bras. At least Kit needed the one she wore. Billie glanced down at her own chest, which, like Hazel's, was as flat as a game board.

She used the handkerchief to pry the disgusting object from her hair, nodding toward the back of the bus. "Those guys are louts."

"Fancy word." Tito nodded appreciatively. "Not sure what it means, but I like the sound of it."

"Awkward and ill-mannered fellows." Billie shook the spit wad from the carefully ironed hanky and kicked it under the seat in front of her. "Describes them to a T."

When Billie turned eleven, her great-aunt Doff deemed her old enough to touch the whisper-thin pages of the ancient dictionary enthroned on the stand in the parlor. *Deemed*—"to give or pronounce judgment"—was another of the words that had snagged Billie's attention. When she peered through the antique bone-handled magnifying glass, she felt like a true explorer, discovering new continents in the worlds of microscopic black-and-white print.

Another spit wad bounced off her saddle shoe. Despite the fact they couldn't hit a target at five paces, the baboons in the back howled even louder. She scooted away from the aisle, closer to her little second-grade seatmate. It would take more than a few spit wads to ruin Billie's day.

The minute her brother stepped on that bus for San Diego, six long weeks ago, Billie had begun her countdown. That first night, the one red *X* on the Feed and Seed calendar looked utterly lonely. But now it had forty-one brothers and sisters. And Leo was on his way home on a weekend pass. She had everything planned: a drive into town, with time on the pier, a picnic out beyond the avocado orchard, and lots of rounds of Criss Cross Words. She was determined to make each moment count.

Leo bragged that once he got to fighting, the Germans and the Japs would hightail it for the hills. "It'll be over like that," he'd said, with a finger snap. But nobody knew when the war might end. Not even Mr. Edward R. Murrow, who'd been covering it since before Uncle Sam got in the fight.

Mr. Murrow's broadcasts were the only ones Doff trusted. Last Sunday, he'd reported live from a C-47 airplane as nineteen American paratroopers parachuted into Holland. Billie held her breath as she listened. "They're getting ready to jump," he'd said in his strong voice. "There they go! Three, four, five . . . Seventeen, eighteen, nineteen!" When he'd described the men dropping down beside a windmill, near a little church, Billie felt she'd been right there with them. She'd hardly slept that night, thinking of those brave soldiers stepping out of a plane, held in the air like tiny spiderlings by those fine silk chutes. Mr. Murrow's reports were enthralling, but Billie had listened to them for three long years. Leo could brag all he wanted, but Billie worried that the war might never end.

The bus bounced past the Stewarts' house, jostling Billie back to the present. There was Stanley riding his trike around his little sister, Didi, clutching her beloved MuMu Monkey. Stanley bumped into his sister and she ran for the house to tattle. It was a situation Billie knew all too well from hours of babysitting those two.

The bus juddered onto the shoulder, wheezing to a stop. Hazel and Kit hopped off, arm in arm. Mrs. French probably had some icebox cookies waiting for them. Though Billie knew why, it still hurt that Hazel had stopped saving seats for her. Stopped wanting to have sleepovers, or debating which was the best Wizard of Oz story. No more cutting pictures out of the Monkey Ward catalog, dreaming of what they'd buy if they had one hundred dollars. Clearly, Hazel had written Billie's name in pencil in her book of life, easy to erase.

After her seatmate got off, Billie slid over to the window, resting her head. Perhaps the jostling would bounce worries about Hazel right out of her mind.

The bus hit a pothole and Billie grabbed the armrest to keep from flying off the seat. A magazine landed in the aisle. *Sky and Telescope*.

She picked it up and handed it to Tito.

"That was a good film strip today." He pushed his glasses up on his nose. "My old school was for Mexican kids only. No film strips. Or even a library."

"Every school has a library!"

Tito peered at her, as if inspecting a strange bug. "One time, some church donated books they'd collected." He shrugged. "Papá says his job for your aunt is an answer to our prayer. A good school for me and good work for him."

"Well, with Leo in the Marines, Doff needed help." Tito's father was the third ranch manager hired since August. No local man would take the job; Doff was that hard to work for. But, after his first week, Mr. Garcia had taken home a jar of Doff's prize-winning preserves. A sure sign of her approval.

"If you like big words, this is for you." Tito held up his magazine. "Would you like to borrow it sometime?"

Through the window, Billie could see Kit and Hazel scurry toward Hazel's house. Did Mrs. French call Kit pumpkin, like she had Billie? Would she serve them milk coffee with their after-school snack? Did Hazel even play the "if I had a hundred dollars game" anymore?

Billie sighed. Surely, there weren't expiration dates on friendship, like there were on ration stamps. There had to be something she could do to be Hazel's friend again.

She realized Tito was waiting for an answer. "No, thank you." She leaned her head against the window glass again. Now she was even more impatient for Leo to get home. He had all kinds of friends. He'd know just what she should do.

CHAPTER TWO

Denny

"I don't get it." Leo wiped his sweaty forehead as another sedan rolled by without stopping. "This uniform is usually a sure ticket for a ride."

Denny stood on the shoulder, considering. Was Leo truly blind to the reasons they hadn't been picked up? That some Anglos would never offer a ride to an Indian, not even one wearing the Marines uniform? His new buddy had no idea what it was like to grow up on the reservation. Being hauled off to boarding school as an eight-year-old, where the main lesson was that being Diné was unacceptable. Ten years later, Denny could still taste the soap the principal would shove in his mouth every time he spoke Navajo, his own language. Fels-Naphtha.

"I hope we get a ride soon." Leo crouched, turning his duffel bag into a makeshift seat. "Doff's probably been knocking herself out, cooking a feast." He rummaged in his shirt pocket and pulled out a pack of Dentyne. "Want a piece of gum?"

Denny shook his head. Something caught his ear and he turned away. "Hear that?" He dropped his own duffel and stepped a few feet in one direction and then another, listening. All those years of watching his mother's sheep had trained him to recognize the sound of an injured animal. He broke into a jog, tracking the whimpers.

"Where are you going?" Leo hollered after him.

"Be right back!" Denny followed a dry creek up a small rise. As he ran down the other side, he spied a patch of black fur. Smelled it, too. Been out there a while. The dog raised its head as Denny approached.

"*Yá 'át'ééh*, friend." He bent down, out of reach, waiting. Watching.

The dog was banged up pretty good. Maybe fell out of the back of a truck. Handsome, despite looking worse for wear.

"Hello, friend," Denny repeated. He took in the upright ears, long muzzle, the blaze of white on his chest. And those brown eyes, dull with the all-too-familiar pain of rejection.

"Looks like we have something in common." In eighteen years, the first time *he'd* felt accepted was at boot camp, where the drill instructors dealt with every single recruit like something to be scraped off a boot. College professor or pipe fitter, the DIs treated everyone the same. But boot camp was also the first time an Anglo had ever complimented him. "I don't get to present many expert awards," the DI had said when Denny got the highest score on the rifle range. He even shook his hand.

Denny eased toward the injured animal. "You need some help."

The dog blinked. Did not bare his teeth. Did not growl. When his eyes met Denny's a second time, something passed between them. A message known to those who are lost or searching. "You've got work to do." Denny stroked the long muzzle and caught the sound of a soft sigh. "All right, then. Let's get out of here."

The dog struggled to stand.

"It's okay, buddy." Denny positioned himself. "I got this." The dog yelped but allowed himself to be cradled in Denny's arms. Though his ribs showed he hadn't eaten in many days, the dog was solid. Healthy, he'd probably weigh fifty pounds, same as the packs they'd carried on training hikes. Denny stumbled a few times as he traversed up and down the rolling terrain, making his way back to the highway.

Leo ran his hand over his close-cropped hair when he saw them. "A dog?"

"He's hurt."

"Not going to help with the ride situation."

"I couldn't leave him."

Leo shook his head. "You and my sister are going to get along like gangbusters. Neither of you ever met a bad idea you didn't like."

Denny struggled to reach down and pick up his duffel.

"I got it." Leo tossed Denny's bag over his free shoulder. "What are you going to do with him when we leave for camp on Sunday?"

Denny didn't answer. Leo took their bags and moved to the edge of the highway. He stuck out his thumb.

A weekend wasn't much time to find a home for the dog. As if reading Denny's mind, the dog licked his hands in a reassuring manner. It was no accident that they'd met. There was a reason.

Ten more cars whizzed by before a traveling salesman pulled onto the shoulder. He threw an old blanket on the backseat and helped Denny ease the dog inside. "He looks like the one I had growing up," the man said. "Bingo. Now, there was a good mutt."

"Do you want him?" Denny asked hopefully.

"I've got five kids," the man said. "That's enough wild creatures for one house." He laughed. "Hop in, boys. I gotta get to San Clemente by suppertime."

CHAPTER THREE

‖‖

Billie

Billie slipped off her book bag and jacket, and reached for one of the oatmeal cookies cooling on the rack.

"Uh, uh, uh." Doff shook her head. "Those are Leo's."

Billie made a big production of pouring herself a glass of milk, stirring in a spoonful of Ovaltine powder. "I guess I'll have plain old saltine crackers for my snack."

Doff basted the turkey roasting in the oven. "When you come home from six weeks at boot camp, you can eat all the cookies you want."

Billie pulled out the Nabisco cracker tin. The smell of the turkey took her back to last Thanksgiving. Doff and Leo had a big fight when Doff refused to sign some paper so he could enlist early. He had slapped his palm on the counter. "You don't understand what it's like to want to help your country."

Doff had slammed the oven door shut. "You have no idea what you're talking about." And though the table was set with all their family favorites, no one enjoyed their holiday meal after that.

It wasn't long after Leo turned eighteen that Uncle Sam's letter arrived. Doff didn't need to sign anything after all. She'd hardly said a word about it until they took Leo to the bus in San Diego. After he got on, she wiped her eyes with a floral hanky, insisting it was the dust making them water. But Billie noticed they watered the entire drive back to the ranch.

Billie crunched the last bite of cracker with a glance at the red metal clock hung over the stove.

"Do you need me for anything?" she asked.

"Not now." Doff closed the oven door, this time without a slam. "You can set the table later. Go change."

In her room, Billie pushed her pigtails to one side to unbutton the back of her school dress. Kit called pigtails "babyish." She'd had her hair bobbed a few days into the school year. Shortly after, Hazel's pigtails were gone, too.

Billie stood in front of the mirror, trying to picture herself with short hair. A feathery flip like Kit and Hazel's meant pin curls every night. Assuming she could bear the inconvenience, how would she look? She turned her head this way and that. Then she stopped, taking a long hard look in the mirror. Who did she take after? Her mother? Her father? A photo of the two of them, on their wedding day, was displayed in an onyx frame on the mantel in the parlor. It'd been taken from such a distance that her parents' faces were mere smudges. But her mother had short hair, worn in the soft Marcel waves of the 1920s. And Doff had told her more than once that her mother was beautiful.

The scissors called to Billie from the top of the dresser. She got a tight grip on her right pigtail. One snip and she'd surely be back in Hazel's good graces. She picked up the scissors, slowly pinching the handles closed. *Snick.* A few strands of brown hair fluttered to the floor. Billie looked down, feeling queasy.

One of Leo's habits was tugging her pigtails. It would be unpatriotic to shock him with a new hairstyle. Billie dropped the scissors, bending to pick up the cut strands of hair. She looked at them for a moment before tossing them in the wastebasket. Keeping her pigtails was the least she could do after all Leo had done for her over the years.

Hadn't he held her hand as she took her first baby steps? And listened to her stumble through the Dick and Jane readers: "Look, Dick. See, Jane."? And when he was thirteen, hadn't he taught her to ride a bike? She had the chipped tooth to prove it. Doff had scared up a hand-me-down Schwinn from somewhere for Billie's sixth birthday. Leo ran up and down the drive that morning, holding on to the back of the bicycle, keeping Billie balanced. Finally, he hollered, "You've got it," and let her go. She pedaled triumphantly down the driveway, buoyed by her brother's confidence. Unfortunately, Leo hadn't given her steering lessons and Billie crashed into a fence post. Doff pooh-poohed away the blood and the chipped tooth, saying, "Bumps and bruises are signs you're really living."

Billie ran her tongue over that uneven front tooth now as she tucked in her blouse. What would it be like to be Hazel, with Mrs. French fussing over her every scratch and scrape? Billie couldn't recall Doff fussing over her. Not once. Maybe it was because she never had kids of her own and didn't know that was something mothers did. Doff's was the brown Oxford kind of love: solid and sensible. No frills.

Billie peeked out her bedroom window. No sign of a car. Leo should've been there by now. Tightening her pigtails, she wandered back to the kitchen. "Should I set the table *now*?" If they got everything ready, he would surely arrive.

"Still a bit early." Doff chunked peeled potatoes into a big pot. "Why don't you get your game set up?" She chuckled. "Leo's going to get shellacked, with the way you've kept your nose in that dictionary."

Doff was right. All that time with the dictionary was going to pay off. For once, Billie was going to outscore Leo! After setting up the board on the parlor game table, she dumped out the letter tiles and began the chore of turning them facedown.

"I see dust!" Doff announced.

Billie dropped the tiles from her hand, skidded through the house and out the front door.

A strange sedan was making its way over the bumps and ruts of the drive. It stopped and a Marine—not Leo—slid out.

"Can I help you?" Doff asked over Billie's shoulder.

Before the Marine could answer, the rear passenger door popped open.

"Leo!" Billie leaped off the porch and ran to her brother, latching herself to his neck.

"Let a guy breathe!" Laughing, he swung her around. She wobbled a bit when her feet touched the ground again, feeling dizzy from sheer happiness. "I hope you ladies don't mind, but I brought a buddy." Leo reached back for a duffel bag and tossed it to the other soldier. "Denny Begay, this is my pesky kid sis and my great-aunt Dorothy Packer."

"Call me Doff." She stuck out her hand. "Glad to have you, Denny."

Billie's heart tumbled from its cozy spot on Cloud Nine. This was her last weekend with Leo.

She knew she was going to have to share him with Doff and Flo. And now there was somebody else? That was the definition of inconsiderate. She glowered at the intruder.

Doff poked her in the back, reminding her of her manners. Billie grunted a greeting to Denny.

"Oh, the pie!" Doff dashed inside.

Leo ducked into the sedan, tugging out another duffel. He tossed it on the ground. "Billie, can you lend a hand?"

"Can't a big strong Marine carry his own dad-blamed bag?" she grumbled.

"That's not what I need your help with." Leo leaned into the backseat once more. After a few seconds, he emerged.

Holding a dog.

CHAPTER FOUR

Denny

Leo's little sister brought an old sheet out to the sun porch. Denny tore it into strips and gently wrapped the dog's torso, exploring each rib as he worked. "This one might be cracked, but not broken."

The girl's face paled with concern.

"He's so skinny." She stroked his head. "Should I get him something to eat?"

"Water first." Denny tied off the last cotton strip.

She hurried away, returning with a chipped blue bowl, water sloshing over the sides. The dog lapped at it.

"Can I give him this?" She held out a cold frankfurter.

"A little bit at a time." Denny eased out of her way. "Don't want to overwhelm his stomach."

She broke the frankfurter into small chunks and held one in the palm of her hand. The dog sniffed, then inhaled it, not even bothering to chew. Leo's sister laughed. "He likes it."

Denny felt up and down each of the dog's legs. "Nothing wrong here," he said. "He'll be chasing cats in no time."

"There's an old curry brush in the barn. I could get those mats out," she said. "Would you like that?" she asked the dog. "Maybe a bath, too?"

By way of answer, the dog nosed at her hand for another bite of meat. She looked over to Denny for the okay, which he gave. "How do you think he got out there?"

"I don't know." Denny took a seat on the wicker chair. "But I have a feeling he was waiting for someone."

"You?" The girl stroked the dog's muzzle.

Denny shook his head. "Someone who can give him a home."

"And you'll be shipping out, like Leo, after Camp Pendleton." The girl's hand paused. "So you can't because of being in the Marines."

A few quiet moments passed and soon the dog was snoring. Denny studied the girl. Leo said they'd have something in common. Maybe they did. He'd decided to trust her with his discovery.

"I've been taking care of my mother's sheep since I could walk." He ran his hands over his thighs, back and forth. A nervous habit he couldn't break. "They're not very good at conversation, sheep, but you spend enough time with them, you start to understand what they're thinking."

Leo's sister stretched out her legs; both big toes poked through her worn Keds. She didn't say anything, but she was listening. Hard.

"I met this dog, and I thought, he's here for a reason." Denny rested his hands on his knees.

The girl turned to him, her face a question mark.

Denny forged ahead. "And I think it's to help you find what you're looking for."

"Are you pulling my leg?" The girl frowned. "Leo does that all the time."

"I'm not a kidder."

The girl's face glowed as if suddenly bathed in candlelight. "I've always wanted a dog." Her face just as quickly darkened. "But I could never convince Doff."

Denny stood and moved to the porch door. "She might surprise you." He rested his hand on the doorknob. "One more thing."

Leo's sister scooted closer to the dog; he stirred, throwing a paw over her leg. "What?"

"His name is Bear."

CHAPTER FIVE

Billie

"Over my dead body." Doff's arms formed an X across her chest. "And I *don't* plan on kicking the bucket anytime soon."

"But we can't turn away an injured creature!" Billie hurried around the table, setting out plates. "It's not Christian!"

"Since when does the Golden Rule apply to animals?"

Billie was glad, for once, that she'd paid attention in Sunday School. "Jesus was a shepherd!"

"Of lambs, not dogs." Doff sprinkled flour into a saucepan on the stove.

"I promise to take care of him." Billie took silverware from the drawer. "You won't have to do anything."

"I've got trouble enough. Some critter's made off with my three best layers." She *thwapped* the whisk around to mix in the flour. "All this chitchat has made my gravy lumpy."

"I promise." Billie held up three fingers. "Scout's honor."

Doff sighed.

Billie held her breath.

Doff sighed again. "It can stay till it's well."

Knives and forks and spoons clattered to the table as Billie ran to hug her great-aunt. "Thank you!"

"I'm sure I'll regret this." Doff pulled the saucepan off the flame. "Go call those boys. Supper—lumpy gravy and all—is ready."

Leo and Denny, freshly showered and dressed in chinos and button-down shirts instead of uniforms, came in from the bunkhouse without being called twice.

"Home-cooked food!" Leo sniffed the air. "Doff makes the best gravy."

"It'll be a treat after the food at camp," Denny added, though he didn't mind the mess hall chow. The sergeant never had to stand over him, making sure he cleaned up his Salisbury steak, or chipped beef, or fried chicken, like he did some of the Anglo boys. All those nights, growing up, going to bed with an empty belly had taught Denny to eat whatever was put in front of him, whenever it was put in front of him.

"I can keep him!" Billie bounced on her chair.

Doff cleared her throat. "Until it's healed up," she clarified.

"He," Billie corrected. "Bear."

"Don't go getting attached." Doff passed Denny a bowl brimming with mashed potatoes.

"Her secret is buttermilk," Leo said. "Best taters ever."

Like Leo and Denny, Billie piled her plate with food as each serving dish passed by.

"Worked up quite an appetite today, did you?" Doff asked.

Billie forked up some string beans. "Well, everything tastes better with Leo home," she said. "And you, too, Denny," she added politely. He'd found Bear, after all. "Would you like to play Criss Cross Words with us after dinner?"

"And interfere with your battle to the death?" Denny passed her the roll basket. "Not on your life."

"He's chicken a kid will beat him," Leo teased.

"Oh, I know she would." Denny broke his roll and began to butter it. "Thanks for the invite, but you two go ahead. I might borrow one of those books I saw in the parlor, if that's all right."

"Dad's favorite author was Jules Verne." That was one thing Billie knew about her father. All the books on the parlor shelves bore bookplates on the inside front cover that said, "Property of Emerson Packer."

"Mine, too." Denny lifted his coffee cup as if toasting Dad's good taste. "I wanted to join the Navy because of *Twenty Thousand Leagues under the Sea*, but Uncle Sam put all us Navajos in the Marines."

"You're Navajo?" Billie had wondered if Denny was an Indian but wasn't sure it was polite to ask.

He nodded. "We call ourselves Diné, which means 'the people.'"

Billie tried the word out. "Dee-neh."

"I'm of the Big-Water Clan," Denny added. "Born for the Red-Cheek-People Clan."

"That sounds like a poem." Billie put her fork down, head cocked to the side. "What does it mean?"

"Don't hound the poor fellow," Doff scolded. "Let him eat in peace."

"It's okay, ma'am." Denny set his fork down, too. "A Navajo baby is born *to* the mother's clan, and *for* the father's clan. We introduce ourselves to other Diné in this way, sometimes even saying the names of our grandparents' clans, so those we meet know where we come from."

"So I would be Billie, born *to* the Radvich clan, and born *for* the Packer clan." She made a face. "That's not as poetic." It didn't feel honest, either. Could you be born to a clan when you'd never met anybody in it? Her own mother had passed away months after Billie was born. That's when Dad brought them to Doff's. It seemed like Denny's family connections ran ocean deep. Hers were summertime mud puddles. "Does everyone, every Diné, wear a pouch like that?"

He tucked a small buckskin bag under the collar of his shirt. "Many do. *Shi cheii*, my grandfather, made this for me." He read from her eyes that she was curious about what was inside. But such things were personal. Private. He could tell her a little something, though. "We use it to carry corn pollen and small tokens," he said.

Leo handed Denny the turkey platter, and at the same time handed Billie a dirty look. It said: *Don't be so nosy.* "Have seconds," he encouraged Denny. "I'm going to."

Billie took a sip of milk, washing down all the other questions she wanted to ask. She wasn't trying to be nosy. It was so interesting. Like how Denny knew things about Bear. How to take care of his wounds. Why Bear was there.

She pushed aside a few bites of turkey. Doff would have conniptions if she caught Billie "wasting perfectly good food on a dog." But Bear needed it to heal up. She nibbled on a green bean, scheming.

"Are there any of those apricot preserves for these rolls?" Leo asked. "I've been dreaming about them for the last six weeks."

Doff scooted her chair out from the table.

"Don't get up." Leo pushed his chair back, too. "Tell me where they are and I'll get them."

"You'd just make a mess of things." Doff's house slippers scuffed across the linoleum floor and down the dark basement steps to the root cellar.

"Now's your chance," Leo said. "Quick."

Billie didn't have to be told twice. "Thanks!" How did Leo know what she'd been thinking?

Bear stirred when she opened the door.

"Hungry?" She tossed the turkey into one of the chipped Blue Willow bowls she'd commandeered for dog dishes. "I brought the works." She scraped potatoes and gravy and green beans over the meat. Bear thumped his tail slowly, watching her. When her plate was empty, she set the bowl under his nose.

Bear ate his supper, then settled back down on the blanket Billie had spread out for him. When she stroked between his eyes, as Denny had done earlier, he snuffled softly. Relaxed.

"Get some rest now." She tiptoed back inside, slipping into her place as Doff *clump-clump-clumped* up the last few steps from the cellar.

"These preserves won the blue ribbon at the county fair." Doff held a gleaming jar aloft. "Sorry to say, this is the last of the batch." She twisted off the metal ring and popped the seal with a church key.

Leo sniffed the contents appreciatively. "Takes me back to summertime." He spooned the shimmering preserves onto his roll. "You better try some." He handed the jar to Denny, then leaned forward, winking at Billie. "Hey, kiddo. Your plate's empty. How about seconds?" He passed her the turkey platter and she took two more slices. One for her. One for Bear.

While Denny dived into *Twenty Thousand Leagues under the Sea*, Billie whupped Leo at Criss Cross Words, five games straight.

"'Inevitable'!" Leo exclaimed as Billie laid down the tiles. "What have you been doing? Memorizing the dictionary?"

Grinning, Billie added up her points. "I won. Again." She clasped her hands over her head like a victorious prizefighter.

"Time for bed, Billie." Doff set down her knitting. Another pair of olive drab socks for the troops.

"Can't we play just one more game?" Billie begged.

"I've got a hot date, squirt." Leo reached across the table and tugged her pigtail. "Flo's expecting me. We can have a rematch tomorrow."

"Well, then, I'll check on Bear." Billie dumped a handful of tiles back into the game box.

"The dog's fine," Doff said firmly.

"We'll get him settled before we go," Leo promised.

Billie wanted to be the one to take care of Bear, but there was no arguing with Doff. "See you in the morning." She gave Leo another hug and then waved to Denny.

He held up the book he was reading. "It's even better the second time."

"Good night, sleep tight," Leo called as she padded down the hall. "Don't let the—"

"—Bedbugs bite." She completed the phrase that he'd been saying to her for as long as she could remember. His chuckle followed her into her room and warmed her like the quilt she tucked herself under. The evening had passed by so quickly, she hadn't had the chance to ask Leo's advice about Hazel. Billie switched off the lamp, shutting out thoughts of Sunday evening and her brother's too-soon departure.

The wind woke her some hours later. She sat up, cleared her foggy head, and listened. That wasn't the wind. And it was too muffled for Doff's snoring. Billie tossed back the covers, shivering as her bare feet hit the cold linoleum floor.

The noise stopped as soon as she stepped onto the sun porch.

"What's wrong?" The strips around Bear's ribs were still snug. She sat by him, back against the wall. "Lonely?" When she stretched out her legs, Bear plunked his head on her lap.

She rubbed his ears, wishing she'd remembered the curry brush from the barn. That would turn this matted black fur soft as silk. She scratched along the white blaze on his chest.

"What happened? Did you get left behind?" She stroked him again and again, trying to wipe away such pain. "Never mind. You're safe now."

Bear cocked his ears. He studied her with the kind of look Hazel used to wear when she and Billie were trading secrets. She never had found the courage to tell Hazel her deepest secret. But she would. As soon as they were friends again.

"Can you really help me find what I most want?" She untangled a knot of black fur with her fingers. Denny had seemed convinced that Bear could. "Shall I tell you what it is?" she whispered. "No one else knows."

Billie had wished on a thousand stars. Written a score of letters that could never be mailed. She'd even entered that jingle contest last spring, certain she'd come up with a winner: "It's evident when you brush with Pepsodent."

Hazel hadn't understood Billie's disappointment when a kid named Terry Shay won with the slogan "Every teen wants the Pepsodent gleam." But she didn't know the real reason Billie had entered the contest. Now, wherever he was; Dad would open a magazine or newspaper and see Terry Shay's face in the Pepsodent advertisement, instead of Billie's. After losing that contest, Billie had nearly given up on trying to get Dad home. It had been ten years. She had no illusions of him staying; he'd probably made a completely new life for himself. All she wanted was to ask him a question. One measly question.

"You're going to help with Dad, aren't you, boy?" She rubbed either side of Bear's muzzle, looking intently into his soft dark eyes. Hours before, she hadn't even known Bear existed; now she couldn't imagine life without him. There was probably a big fancy word for that somewhere in Doff's dictionary.

But there was a simpler word, too.

Billie curled up on the floor, cradling her head in her right arm. She twined the fingers of her left hand in Bear's thick black fur, holding tight as if she would never let go.

‖‖‖‖‖‖‖‖‖‖‖‖‖‖‖‖‖‖‖‖‖‖‖‖‖‖‖‖‖‖‖‖‖‖‖‖‖‖

CHAPTER SIX

Billie

A cold wet nose tapped Billie's cheek. She thrashed around, trying to sit up. Then she remembered where she was. On the sun porch. With Bear.

"Good morning." His left leg thumped as she rubbed along his spine. "Does that feel good?" When she stood to stretch out a few of her own kinks, Bear got up, too, then went to the door.

"Oh, you need out. Let me find a leash." She didn't see a rope or old belt or anything. What had Leo and Denny used? "I'll be right back," she promised.

She ran full speed past the abandoned corral to the bunkhouse. "Leo! Wake up!" She pounded on the door.

Her brother appeared, yawning. "Where's the fire?"

"What did you use for a leash last night?" Billie put her hands on her hips. "I have to walk Bear."

"Oh." Another yawn. "Hang on." He disappeared, returning with a length of light rope.

She grabbed it and ran back. "Here I am!" she called.

But the sun porch was empty.

"Bear?"

There was nowhere for him to hide. And she'd shut the door tight behind her. He couldn't have opened it by himself. Billie ducked her head into the kitchen. "Have you seen Bear?"

"Pancakes will be ready soon." Doff sprinkled water on the griddle. It sizzled. "That dog practically scratched through the door. So I let him out."

Billie's heart sank. "Without a leash?"

"I didn't see hide nor hair of you, Miss I-Promise-to-Take-Care-of-Him." Doff tipped a bowl over the griddle, pouring out four circles of batter.

"But what if he tries to cross the highway?" Billie asked. "Or doesn't come back?" Her throat was so tight with worry that it was painful to ask such questions.

"That dog's got sense enough not to run in front of cars." Doff set a syrup pitcher on the table. "Now go call those boys to breakfast, will you?"

Billie bit her lip to keep from saying things that might get her sent to her room. But she did slam the screen door, hard, behind her.

Leo was on the bunkhouse porch, tugging on a clean shirt. "What's with the long face?"

"Doff let Bear out." Billie flung the rope at him. "I don't know where he is."

Leo jumped down the steps and was at her side in an instant, his arm around her shoulder. "He'll be back. He's got a good thing here."

She leaned close, inhaling Black Jack gum and Barbasol aftershave, wishing she could bottle this smell to keep her company while he was gone.

Leo gave her a squeeze, then stepped away to finish buttoning his shirt. "You've got nothing to worry about."

Leo was wrong. She had plenty to worry about. It wasn't just losing Bear. She picked at a sliver of wood on the railing. Of course, her brother didn't know about Hazel.

She crumbled the sliver between her fingers. "Where's Denny?"

"Out for a run. I guess he didn't get enough of that in boot camp." Leo tucked in his shirttails. "Breakfast ready?"

Billie nodded. "Pancakes."

He tugged on her pigtail. "I guess I better be polite and leave at least one stack for Denny."

"Where's Denny?" Doff glanced up from her cooking as they entered the kitchen.

"That's what Billie asked, too." Leo made a face. "What am I? Chopped liver?"

Doff waved her spatula at him. "You're too big for your britches, is what you are." She slid some pancakes into the oven to keep warm before serving Leo.

Billie traced figure eights with her fork on her plate. "Can I go look for Bear? I'll be back by lunchtime."

"It's 'May I,'" Doff corrected.

"May I?" Billie asked.

Doff poured a cup of coffee and handed it to Leo. "After breakfast."

"I'm not hungry."

"I thought we had a date to go into town this morning." Leo added some cream to his coffee. "Flo's counting on you coming along."

Last night, Billie had planned to take every penny of the three dollars and seventy-nine cents in her piggy bank to buy Bear a proper collar and leash and other dog supplies in town. No point in it now.

"Speaking of Flo, you're not thinking to be another Patty and Ed, are you?" Doff asked.

"Do you mean do I plan to get hitched before I ship out?" Leo grinned. "And deprive you and Flo's mom of the chance to plan a big shindig? Nothin' doing."

"Well, at least you're being sensible." Doff grumbled. "Eighteen-year-olds have no business getting married."

"How old were you when you walked down the aisle?" Leo winked at Billie. "Oh, yes. Now I remember. Eighteen."

Doff snapped a dish towel at him. "Those were different times. Folks married younger." She got up and went to the stove, reaching for the percolator handle.

"These are different times, too. What with the war." Leo's face got serious. "I wish Patty and Ed all the best, but I couldn't do that to Flo. Marry her, and then ship out. What if something happened?"

Doff's hand froze in midair.

Leo jumped up and went to her. "I didn't mean—" A look passed between the two of them. Then he kissed the top of her gray head, and took the coffee-pot from her to refill their mugs.

They didn't realize it, but Billie knew what was going on. It was the reason Doff had been so stub-born about signing Leo's papers. The reason she'd cried all the way back from the bus station the day Leo left for boot camp.

Billie hadn't meant to pry. She'd only been look-ing for a stamp to send Leo a letter. There weren't any in the empty Folgers tin in the kitchen, so she checked the secretary in the parlor. The first drawer she opened was crammed with old papers. On the very bottom of the mess, she found some stamps along with a dozen tissue-thin pieces of mail, tied up with blue ribbon. The first two were addressed to 'My darling Doff,' signed 'Your loving Hugh,' with a lot of mushy stuff in between. The worst was when Hugh had written, 'I long to kiss those cherry-sweet lips of yours.' Billie couldn't imagine Doff kissing anyone. As she had started to put the letters away, she noticed a telegram on the bottom of the stack. It was dated August 12, 1918: *"Deeply regret to inform you that Private Hugh Packer Infantry is reported as killed in action July ninth. Harris, the Adjutant General."*

Doff's "loving Hugh," their great-uncle, had never made it home from the war. Billie had known he'd died long before they showed up, but Doff never said how. And Billie had never asked.

"Why don't you sit?" Leo carried their cups back to the table. "I can handle the rest of the flapjacks."

Doff stared into space as if time had stopped, her coffee untouched. "Leo?" She finally spoke, picking up her mug.

"Yeah?" He studied the pancakes, looking like he was trying to decide whether to turn them over or not.

Doff's hand went to her mouth, covering lips that were wrinkled and chapped and nothing like cherries. She shook her head. Sighed. "Don't flip them till the bubbles start popping."

"Sir, yes, sir!" Leo snapped off a salute, spatula in hand.

Even though Doff smiled at Leo's attempt at humor, Billie knew what she was thinking. *She* was thinking the same thing.

Don't let what happened to Hugh happen to Leo.

CHAPTER SEVEN

Denny

His mother had awakened him before dawn since he could remember, sometimes throwing him in winter's first snow to toughen him up, sometimes urging him to run east as far and fast as he could. His grandmother said these customs started after the Long Walk, when so many People perished. Every Diné mother wanted her children strong enough to survive should such an atrocity ever happen again.

Though Denny had spent all of boot camp working to become more Marine and less Navajo, some habits died hard. He could not help awakening at dawn each day. Could not stop himself from immediately facing east.

He stretched his calf muscles and began to run toward the rising sun. Maybe it was for the best that Grandfather couldn't write. If he did, he would ask about morning prayers. Honor would command that Denny answer truthfully. *Cheeii* would be disheartened to know that he had given them up during boot camp. Sometimes being a Marine felt more comfortable than being Diné. It was certainly more acceptable in the Anglo world.

Denny loped past the empty barn and corral, Doff's Victory Garden, the chicken coops, through the avocado orchards and beyond.

Leo had been the only one in their platoon able to match his pace during the training runs. Strap forty or fifty pounds to their backs and they still led the way. It was on the overnight run that Denny had shown Leo which plants could quench their thirst. The DI scratched his head when the two of them returned with nearly full canteens, and the rest of the men arrived dizzy from dehydration.

He increased his speed when he hit scrub prairie and rocky patches reminding him of home. But the air held not a whiff of sheep or goats. When would he smell that again? Would he return from the war when his mother's flock was in the summer corral? At shearing time? Or would he be one of those who did not come home? Before Denny left for boot camp, Grandfather gave a Blessingway ceremony to ensure his safe return. From the war. To the reservation. Grandfather would be praying for both.

Stickers of doubt pricked with each step. There were so many names of the fallen printed in the papers each month. Grandfather's prayers *might* ensure Denny's safe return from the fighting, but a return to the reservation was another thing. The DI and one of the sergeants had already talked to Denny about staying in. Making the Marines a career.

Like a desert freshened by a spring rain, that thought renewed him; he broke into a confi-dent sprint, looping around a rock outcropping that looked like an enormous creature—an elephant, maybe, but bigger. When he reached the highway, he turned and discovered he was not alone.

Loping toward him was a big black dog, pink tongue flapping as he bounded along.

Denny held up, waited for Bear to catch him. "Exploring your new home?" Denny scratched behind the dog's ears, then patted his thigh. "Coming?"

The dog followed Denny as Denny followed the quiet highway for half a mile or so. By the time they turned west to head back to the ranch, they hadn't seen one vehicle pass by.

Though Bear lagged behind a bit, his stride was even. No limp. "You're nearly healed," Denny observed aloud. Ahead he could see the ranch manager's house. Leo had told him it was about a mile from Rancho Vecinos. Denny slowed his pace; there was still a good distance to run and Bear should take it easy.

Bear seemed to appreciate this act of consideration. He trotted so close that his fur brushed Denny's leg. Together they pushed on as the rising sun melted like butter over the pink sky.

"We need to talk." Fatigue pushed the words out in short bursts. "Billie needs you, and you need a home." Denny breathed deep to find his rhythm. "But there's Doff." Another deep breath. "Time's running out. We gotta get a plan."

Bear barked in agreement, then veered away, increasing his speed.

"Where are you going, mutt?" Denny's stomach grumbled. It demanded breakfast. Time to be getting back.

Then he saw the skinny kid wearing glasses.

He looked like a little owl.

Bear ran onto the porch at the ranch manager's house to introduce himself to the boy, who gave Bear a proper greeting.

"Are you Leo's friend?" the owl-boy called. "Doff told my father about you."

Denny slowed, nodded. Bear was now on his back, eyes closed, as the boy rubbed his furry belly.

"I'm Tito."

Denny noticed a slim blue book tucked under Tito's arm. "I'm Denny and this is Bear."

"What are the strips of cloth for?" Tito asked. Denny told him about finding Bear, and his injuries.

"I hope Billie gets to keep him," Tito said. "She seems lonely."

Smart kid. "What's that book there?" Denny

asked. The smell of frying tortillas wafted out from the house, taking him right back home.

Tito showed him the cover: *Seeing Stars.* "I want to be an astronomer when I grow up."

He nodded at Tito's statement. Let someone else tell this owlish boy that Mexican kids rarely got to college, let alone became astronomers.

"Someone had put this out by their trash." Tito opened the book, showing Denny some of the illustrations inside. "Aren't these beautiful?" He pointed to a drawing. "That's my favorite. Cassiopeia's Chair."

"In Navajo, we call that star—" Denny pointed to the page. "Northern Fire."

"Astronomers call it the North Star. Or Polaris." Tito jumped up. "Are you thirsty? Mamá is squeezing orange juice." He'd already opened the front door.

Denny considered. "I could go for something to drink." He sat on the porch steps and waited. Tito came back with a glass of juice and a little sister. "This is Isabella. I have to watch her while Mamá finishes breakfast."

Isabella blinked big brown eyes at Denny.

"How old are you?" Denny asked in his softest voice.

Isabella hid behind her brother. "She's nearly two," Tito answered for her, turning back to the page with Cassiopeia's Chair. "Tell me more constellation names."

Denny drained the glass and set it down. "That is Northern Female," he said. "See, she's lying on her side." He pointed. "She and Northern Male—or the Big Dipper—represent the family. And Northern Fire represents the fire in the hogan."

"Hogan?" Tito asked.

Denny patted the porch beneath him. "Home."

"I like that," Tito said. "So the family up there keeps the man in the moon company."

"Something like that." Denny bent to unlace one shoe, tying the ends of the lace together. He twisted his fingers through the loop to start the It-Is-Twisted game, which is how his grandmother taught him the stories behind the stars.

"Cat's cradle!" Tito exclaimed.

"Sort of." Denny flipped his fingers over and around the string. "This is Bird's Nest." He flipped again. "Here is Butterflies and"—more flipping.

Isabella's curiosity won out over her shyness. She leaned against Tito, brown eyes intent, as Denny made yet another shape with the loop of string. "And this is Coyotes-Running-Apart."

From inside the house, a woman's voice called out in Spanish.

"We've got to go in now. Thanks for showing us that game." Tito took Isabella's hand. "See you around, Denny. Bye, Bear." As he opened the door, Isabella turned to give Denny a shy wave, which he returned before bending to re-lace his shoe. He tied it snugly, then reached over to pat Bear. "Ready to go?" A bit of black fur stuck to his moist hand. He was about to brush it off when he had a different idea. Rubbing his fingers together, like his mother used to do when she was spinning wool, he turned the bit of fluff into fiber and placed it in the buckskin pouch at his neck.

As he pulled the rawhide string taut to close up the pouch, his stomach complained again, louder this time.

He patted Bear again. "Do you think we're too late for breakfast?"

Bear jumped up and began to run.

"Right." Denny picked up his pace. "Only one way to find out!"

CHAPTER EIGHT

||||||||||||||||||||||||||||||||||||||||||||||||||||||

Billie

Denny stepped into the kitchen, hair damp from a shower. "Sorry I'm late."

"Sit. Sit." Doff fixed him up with coffee and flapjacks.

Billie forced down a bite. "*Now* may I be excused?"

"When everyone's finished," Doff said.

"Don't wait around on my account." Denny reached for the butter.

Doff frowned at Billie. "We do have manners here."

"Bear got out." Billie knew Denny would understand how she was feeling. "I don't know where he is."

He gestured with his fork. "Right outside. We met up while he was out exploring the ranch."

"What?" Billie shoved her chair back.

"I told you he knew he had a good thing here," Leo said.

"There are starving children in China." Doff pointed at Billie's plate. "Didn't I say that dog would be a nuisance?"

"Now that he's back, will you come to town with us?" Leo asked.

"You bet." Billie gobbled the rest of her breakfast. Of course she was going to town. She had pet supplies to buy! "First, Bear needs breakfast!"

It was Denny's first time at the beach, so Billie coaxed him into wading under the pier. Flo and Leo sat on the sand, talking and sharing the occasional kiss when they thought Billie wasn't looking. Lunch was grilled cheese sandwiches at the drugstore lunch counter, followed by a visit to the pier's amusement arcade. At the shooting gallery, some teenage boys kept calling Denny "Chief," and whooping it up like movie Indians. They were louts, like Spinner and Del, only bigger, and Billie wished Leo would say something to them. She tugged on his arm.

"Watch this, sis," he whispered.

Denny lifted the air rifle and aimed at the paper targets.

"Three bull's-eyes in a row!" exclaimed the man behind the counter. "I've never seen the like."

Leo nodded at the boys. "Cat got your tongues?"

They elbowed each other and scuttled off.

"That was terrific!" Billie wasn't sure which she had enjoyed more, watching Denny hit the bull's-eyes or those boys eating humble pie.

"Hitler and crew better watch out for Dead-Eye Denny!" Flo teased.

"Yeah, well, I don't know how much shooting I'm going to do." He offered the prize, a box of chocolates, to Flo. "Uncle Sam's training me as a radio man."

For the past few hours, Billie had almost been able to forget that her brother and his friend were going off to war.

Leo tugged her pigtail. "I bet some ice cream would wipe that frown off your face." He took Flo's arm. "Anyone else? My treat!"

Billie decided to match Leo's good cheer. "How about a root beer float?"

"Anything for you, squirt." He led the way out of the arcade.

"Oh, wait!" Flo dragged Leo over to the nearby glass-enclosed booth. "First, let's get our fortunes."

When Billie was little, this automated fortune-teller had given her the willies. Now she thought it a waste of a perfectly good dime. As always, Madame Zelda moved jerkily inside her case, tinny voice calling out, "Will your luck be good? Will your luck be bad? Madame Zelda knows all!"

Flo slid a coin in the slot and, after much clanking and clanging, a slip of paper popped out. Flo blushed as she read it aloud: "True love finds a way."

Leo waggled his eyebrows like Groucho Marx and she flapped her hand at him. "Now it's your turn," she said.

Leo pretended to grab a fortune from the dispensing slot, holding an imaginary piece of paper in his hand and reading aloud: "Your life belongs to Uncle Sam." He laughed.

"Oh, you!" Flo kissed him on the cheek.

"Are you going to get your fortune?" Denny asked Billie.

She patted her dungarees pocket. "My money's going for a leash and collar."

"Oh, come on." Leo flipped her a coin.

Billie caught it. "I could buy a war stamp with this," she said. With Leo in the Marines, she'd been even more determined to take a dime to school each week. It took eighteen dollars and seventy-five cents' worth of stamps to fill one book, which you could trade in for a twenty-five-dollar savings bond. Billie had done the math. At ten cents a week, she'd be graduating from eighth grade before she earned that bond. No dime-wasting for her.

"It's a lousy ten cents." Leo snatched the coin back and put it in the slot.

Madame Zelda twitched around in her glass booth, waving her mechanical arms: "Will your luck be good? Will your luck be bad? Madame Zelda knows all." The machine workings clacked and clanged as they had moments earlier when Flo inserted her dime. Leo snagged the fortune that slid out. He read: "Someone close to you will go on a journey."

The hairs popped up on Billie's arm. How did this automated fortune-teller know about Leo leaving for Camp Pendleton?

Leo laughed. "Madame Zelda can't go wrong with that prediction, not with so many guys still going off to fight." He tucked his arm through Flo's again. "Now let's go get that ice cream."

A few doors away from the café, Billie paused. "I'm going to duck in here," she said, pointing to the Feed and Seed. "Catch up with you in a few minutes."

"Don't be too long," Leo warned. "Or I might drink your root beer float."

She had never shopped for pet supplies before, but she knew exactly where they were kept at the back of the store. Mr. Baumann never changed any of his displays.

Billie chose a brown leather collar that seemed like it would fit Bear's neck. Then she looked at the price. A dollar ninety-five! She rummaged through the bin, looking for something cheaper. No luck. And leashes cost even more. The price tag for a box of Milk-Bones was thirty-nine cents. Her life's savings weren't going to go far.

"Hello!" Tito stepped out of the tool aisle. "Is that for Bear?" He pushed his glasses up his nose. "I met him this morning. With Denny."

Billie swallowed down her irritation. Bear was *her* dog. Denny was *her* brother's friend. "Well, they were out exploring the ranch." The leash went back on the shelf. She picked up the box of Milk-Bones.

"You don't need a leash?" Tito asked.

She made a face. "Gotta do a little more saving up."

"I—" Tito started, but Kit came around the corner, juggling a handful of seed packets.

"Fancy meeting you two." She tossed her head, pin curls bouncing this way and that.

Billie shifted while Tito said hello. "You're Kit, right?" he asked.

"Guilty as charged," she said, using a line Billie had heard in a movie a while back.

"It looks like you're going to do some planting," Tito said.

Kit held up the packets. "For my Victory Garden."

Tito scanned them. "It might be a little early for those. You probably want to wait until January, and then start with broccoli, cabbage, and carrots."

"Isn't it lucky I ran into him?" Kit turned to Billie. "I guess I should take his advice. Daddy says all the greasers have green thumbs."

She said it so sweetly, Billie almost missed the insult. But Tito didn't. Hurt flashed across his face.

"I guess they didn't teach manners at your old school." Billie's voice quavered as she spoke. How could Kit say such a thing? And to a classmate.

Kit's eyes narrowed. A beat passed. Then she placed her hand on Billie's arm. "I'll be sure and tell Hazel I saw you. I'm going to a sleepover there tonight." Her words carved Billie out like a Halloween jack-o'-lantern. As Kit flounced off, Billie hugged the Milk-Bones box to her chest.

What did Hazel see in her beyond that fluffy hair? Billie turned to Tito. "Doff thinks your dad is such a hard worker and your mom has fixed up the manager's house so cute—"

Tito waved his hand. "You don't need to do that." He shrugged. "Sticks and stones. Sticks and stones."

"But—"

"Papá's probably waiting for me to help load the truck."

Billie watched Tito make his way to the back of the store. Maybe Kit didn't throw spit wads or cause bruises like the louts, but she left marks all the same. Billie paid for the dog biscuits and collar, then ran to the café. She hopped onto a red stool next to Flo.

"What took you?" Leo slid an icy glass, brimming with root beer float, down the counter to her. "Did you run into your boyfriend?"

"Don't answer that!" Flo held up her hand, signaling *stop*. "A girl needs her secrets."

Billie played along. "Loose lips sink ships!" She scooped up a bite of ice cream as Denny and Leo laughed. After another bite, she pushed the glass away. The encounter with Kit had taken away her taste for anything sweet.

Dusk was swiping splotches of gray across the blue sky by the time they headed home. Billie wrapped the dog collar around her wrist like a bracelet and sat in the backseat, turning it around and around.

She had yet to think of a way to convince Doff to let her keep Bear. Billie couldn't afford to take care of a dog on her own, not with one dollar and some change in savings. And Doff didn't believe in paying an allowance for ranch chores. She thought being family meant pitching in. Billie was still chewing over ideas when they pulled up in front of the house.

She and Denny hopped out of the carryall, and Leo drove off, taking Flo home. The long way home, was Billie's guess. "There'll be sandwiches in the kitchen," she told Denny as they climbed the front porch steps. "Help yourself."

"I believe I will." He held the door open for her. "And then I'm going to settle in with that book. I want to finish it before we go."

His words were another prick at Billie's heart. She tucked the Milk-Bones under one arm so she could put her hands on her hips in a Superman pose. "I wish I had the power to slow down time."

Denny's forehead wrinkled. "I don't understand."

"That way the weekend wouldn't go by so fast." She sighed. "I'm really going to miss Leo."

"Thank you for making me feel so welcome. Especially when I know you were counting on time with Leo." Denny loosened the ties on the pouch that he wore around his neck and pulled out a beautiful blue stone. "My father gave this turquoise to me." He held it out. "I want you to have it."

Billie set down the Milk-Bones box. She cupped her hands, as if receiving a communion wafer. "Thank you." The stone felt cool. And surprisingly heavy for its size. "Thank you," she repeated.

"Leo will come home, Billie." Denny's words were a statement of fact. A promise. "Now, I hear a sandwich calling my name."

Billie turned the stone over and over in her hand. Was it magic? Would it grant her three wishes? Tonight, she'd settle for one. She kicked off her Keds in the entryway. "Doff?" she called.

"In here," Doff replied. "Reading."

Billie followed Doff's voice to the parlor. And then stopped in her tracks.

There, curled up at Doff's feet, was Bear.

CHAPTER NINE

Billie

At the knock at her bedroom door, Billie snapped off her lamp.

Leo stepped inside. "Caught ya." He turned the light back on.

"I thought you were Doff." She pulled her pillow onto her lap.

"Some things don't change." Leo tsk-tsked.

"At least I never sneaked out at night." Billie folded her arms across her chest.

"Thanks for keeping *that* secret." Leo reached over and tugged Billie's pigtail. "I still can't get over her taking to Bear. Of course, any creature that saves one of her precious chickens from a raccoon is guaranteed bed and board for life."

"If he's such a hero, why isn't he allowed in the house?" Doff was adamant that Bear's place was on the sun porch. And not one step farther. The moment in the parlor had been an exception. His reward for rescuing Doff's prize Rhode Island Red.

"She may ease up." Leo motioned for Billie to move so he could sit on the edge of the bed. "You doing okay, sis?"

Billie punched her pillow several times. "Fine. Why?"

Leo stretched his legs out. "I wanted to make sure we had time to talk. Just the two of us." He glanced at his watch. "We've got an hour."

Billie's feelings roller-coastered through her gut. She'd thought if she was asleep when Leo left, it wouldn't be so painful. She traced the pattern of her chenille bedspread. "What's there to talk about?" She gritted her teeth against a tidal wave of sad. There was nothing to talk about except everything. After another four weeks of training, her brother was going to war.

"I wanted you to be the first to know." Leo cleared his throat. "I proposed to Flo."

Billie drew her knees up to her chest. "You promised Doff you weren't going to be like Patty and Ed."

Leo patted her leg. "We're not getting married until I get back."

Billie sniffled. "Doff's still going to have conniptions."

"Well, she's going to have to get in line behind Flo's mom."

Biting her lip wasn't enough to stop a tear from plopping onto the bedspread, turning the dot of pink chenille dark red.

"Hey, no waterworks. You'll always be my best girl, squirt."

She forced a smile. "When's the big day?"

"Flo said fifteen minutes after the war ends." He laughed. "She wants me to have something to come home for."

More tears stung Billie's eyes. Wasn't she enough reason to come home? But she already knew the answer to that question. "I like Flo."

"She thinks you're swell, too." He shifted on the bed. "Will you look out for her? Maybe ask Doff to invite her to dinner once in a while?"

Billie nodded. "Sure."

They sat quietly for a few moments. Leo scratched the back of his neck. "If we were in a movie, this would be the scene where I would give you some pearls of wisdom before I depart."

"You? Wisdom? Har-har." Billie worked to keep her tone light.

He elbowed her. "I've taught you a thing or two," he said.

She almost kept the teasing going, almost said something about the chipped tooth from the bike-riding lessons. But she didn't have the heart for it. "Yes, you have." She studied a crack on the ceiling. "You are the best big brother. Ever."

"Okay. So. Well." Leo reached into his pocket and pulled out a small, slim package. "This is for you."

"I didn't get you anything—"

"This isn't from me. Exactly."

"Then who's it from?" She turned the messily wrapped package around in her hands. "And what is it?"

"Why don't you open it, goofball? Then you'll know."

Under the crumpled paper was an emerald-green fountain pen. A Parker Vacumatic.

"It's beautiful." She scribbled in the air. "Perfect for writing letters."

"And I'd better be getting lots." Leo nudged her leg. "But take it easy on those twenty-dollar words from the dictionary. I'm not as brainy as you."

"Don't worry. It'll be Dick and Jane, all the way." She uncapped the pen. The brass nib came to a fine point, a mirror image of the arrow design on the pen clip. "Did Flo help you pick this out?"

Leo didn't answer right away. Then he cleared his throat. "It was Dad's."

"Dad's?" Billie nearly dropped it. This pen had belonged to her father? Had he used it to inscribe his name in all those books in the parlor?

"I found it in his room after—" Leo paused.

"Maybe it belongs to Doff." Billie slid the cap back over the nib, pressing until it clicked.

"I asked her." Leo crumpled the wrapping paper into a tight ball. "It doesn't."

"Do you think he left it—" Billie lowered her voice. "On purpose?" Maybe he'd hoped that one day it would be Billie's. Tears pooled up in her eyes once again.

Leo pulled a hanky from his pocket and handed it over. "I like to think he did." He stood while she wiped her eyes and blew her nose. "You've got school tomorrow. I better let you get some sleep."

She held out the damp hanky.

"Keep it." He opened his arms and she dived in for a Black Jack and Barbasol hug. She drew the deepest breath she could, determined to hang on to this smell. "I'll be gone by the time you get up."

She buried her face in his chest. "I'm going to write you every day!"

He squeezed and let go. "I don't expect every day. But there'd better be letters."

Were those tears glittering in his eyes? Billie swallowed. "We're going to be fine," she assured him. "You're going to be fine."

"Remember. Fifteen minutes after I get home." He tugged her pigtail one last time. "You might want to start looking for a new dress."

She was suddenly very tired. She lay down on the bed, yawning.

He pulled the covers up to her chin, leaned forward, and kissed her on the forehead. He switched off the light.

"Leo?"

"Yeah, squirt?"

She turned her face to the wall. She wanted to say: Please take good care of yourself. Please don't be like Uncle Hugh. Please come home, like Denny said you would. "That's nice about you and Flo."

"I think so, too." He moved toward the door. "Good night, sleep tight and—"

Billie's voice was a whisper. "Don't let the bedbugs bite."

CHAPTER TEN

Denny

September 29, 1944

"Yá'át'ééh!" Keith Little called as Denny stepped inside the communications classroom where they'd spent eight hours and more each day for the past week.

The room was set up like those at boarding school, with a blackboard up front and desks in strict rows. But this blackboard was covered with Navajo words, something that never would have happened in boarding school. Anytime Denny had spoken his own language back then, the teacher wedged a bar of Fels-Naphtha soap in his mouth. Merely thinking about it got the saliva gushing. Denny swallowed down the memories and then grinned at one of the words on the board: *lei-cha-ih-yil-knee-ih*. Dogfaces. Army.

"Hey, cousin." Wilson patted his belly. "Thanks for sharing those cookies last night."

The care package Billie and Doff had sent was a big hit. By the time it got passed around, there were only crumbs for Denny. He was happy to share. With a nod at Sam Holiday and Jesse Smith, he took a seat. Unlike boot camp, there was not one white face in the room.

Denny settled into a desk. "That's a bit of a change." He indicated the blackboard. All week, they'd studied how to send messages in various ways, from semaphores to Morse code. "*Gini.*" He read the Navajo word for chicken hawk. And there was *ne-as-jah*, owl. "We studying birds now?"

"Looks that way," Jesse agreed.

The door swung open and Denny's knee jostled the desk as he hopped to attention. Eighteen sets of chair legs scraped the floor while an Anglo officer strode in, followed by two other Marines. Both Diné.

The Anglo introduced himself in Navajo. Not fluent Navajo, but good enough to get by at the trading post. "Take a seat, gentlemen," Sergeant Johnston ordered.

They did as instructed.

The Anglo turned to one of the Diné officers. "Sergeant Manuelito, would you please get the door?"

Manuelito pulled a set of keys from his pocket and efficiently, purposefully, locked the classroom. The tumbler thunked like an animal trap.

Denny shot a glance over at Jesse, whose forehead wrinkled imperceptibly.

Sergeant Johnston picked up a pointer and tapped at the list of words on the blackboard. "Begay, what's this?" The pointer landed on *ga-gih*.

"Crow," Denny answered.

"That's what it meant yesterday. Today, it means patrol plane." The pointer kept tapping. *Tas-chizzie*, swallow, was a torpedo plane. *Atsah*, eagle, a transport plane.

As the sergeant went down the list, Denny's heart beat faster. It was a code. The Navajo language was the basis of a code. That's why he was here. He glanced around the room. That's why they were all here.

Sergeant Johnston cleared his throat. "From this moment on, nothing that you do or hear in this room leaves this room. Under penalty of imprisonment. Nothing." He stared down the rows of Marines. "Do I make myself clear?"

.Despite the hodgepodge of feelings he was experiencing—bewilderment, curiosity, fear—Denny had been in the Marines long enough to know there was only one possible response to the sergeant's question. At the top of his lungs, he answered with the rest of the men: "Yes, sir!"

PART TWO

"Wishing to be friends is quick work,
but friendship is a slow-ripening fruit."
—Aristotle

CHAPTER ELEVEN

|||||||||||||||||||||||||||||||||||||||||||||||||||||||||||

Billie

October 16, 1944

Billie uncapped the fountain pen and pulled out a clean sheet of paper.

Dear Leo,

It's too bad you and Denny don't get to see each other much. He said he's real busy with communication school. I know, because I've gotten two letters from him and only one from you (hint, hint). Doff and I baked cookies again. You should get them before you ship out. Everyone's guessing that you're going to the Pacific, but I know you can't tell us or you'll get in trouble with the censors.

Be sure to share the cookies with Denny.

Flo came over on Sunday to listen to Mr. Murrow's news reports. She invited us to have Thanksgiving with her family. Doff's going to teach me to make cloverleaf rolls.

I hardly need to use that leash you left for me (thanks, by the way. I sure didn't expect two going-away presents from you). Bear comes every time I call. And he meets me when I get off the bus every afternoon.

Doff's voice bounced down the hall. "You better skedaddle or you'll be late!"

Billie scribbled a few last sentences, signed her name, and sealed the envelope.

Bear followed her down the drive toward the highway. Halfway there, Tito caught up with them, holding out a foil-wrapped packet. "Abuelita made extra tortillas this morning. I brought you one."

Billie unwrapped the packet and took a bite. "Thanks." Warmth flooded her mouth. "I love cinnamon." She tore off a piece from the edge to share with Bear.

"You should make him earn that," Tito said.

"What do you mean?" Billie paused.

"Teach him a trick."

"Okay. Like what?" she asked.

"How about 'stay'?" Tito motioned toward the piece of tortilla. "Break that up smaller. Use it as a reward."

Billie looked at Bear. "Stay." She motioned with her hand. Bear cocked his head at her.

"Now wait a few seconds and then give him the tortilla."

Billie did as Tito suggested. By the time the tortilla was gone, Bear had "stay" down pat.

"That was fun."

"He's a smart dog," Tito said. "I bet you could teach him just about anything."

"A regular Rin Tin Tin." Billie chuckled as she smoothed out the tinfoil. "I can add this to the ball in the classroom." The fifth graders were collecting tinfoil from gum and candy wrappers to donate to the war effort.

They reached the highway as the bus pulled into view. "I'll see you after school," she said. Bear blinked mournfully and stayed put. "Not stay," she said. "Home." She made her voice stern. Bear snuffled in protest, but obeyed, heading back down the drive.

"Sometimes I leave the room for a minute and when I come back, he acts like I've been gone a year."

"I don't think dogs have a good sense of time," Tito observed.

Billie stepped back from the shoulder as the school bus rattled to a stop. "Doff says Bear is the president of the Billie Packer fan club."

"That's funny." Tito smiled. "It must be nice to have such a loyal friend."

When the bus doors swooshed open, Tito stood back to let her on first.

Hazel and Kit were sharing a seat as always, reminding Billie of Tito's words. Bear was a loyal friend. But a girl wanted a human friend, too.

"Hi, Hazel." She paused in the aisle. "That's a nice sweater."

"It matches mine." Kit opened her coat for proof. "They're called twinsets," she said.

Billie continued down the aisle, sliding onto the first free seat, next to Stanley Stewart. Tito passed her, taking a seat with Emil Thompson.

She tried to keep from watching Kit and Hazel, but couldn't help herself. The way they acted, you'd think they'd been friends their whole lives. Not a few months. And where did Hazel get the money for a new sweater set? Billie knew things were tight in the French household.

"Want a Mike and Ike?" Stanley held the candy out in his sweaty hand.

"No, thanks." Billie settled her book bag on her lap.

"I got a letter from Poppa." Stanley popped the Mike and Ike in his mouth. "Only to me," he added, smacking the candy. "Didi cried."

"I bet he wrote her one, too." Billie tightened the ribbons around her pigtails. "Mail can be slow."

"That's what Momma said." Stanley shrugged. "Anyway, Poppa said he was going to bring me—just me—a special souvenir."

"That'll be nice," Billie said. "Did he tell you what it was?"

Stanley concentrated on finishing the Mike and Ike. He swallowed. "No. But Didi can't play with it. Or touch it."

Billie shook her head. Stanley was on a tear today. "Well, you say hi to your mother and Didi for me, okay?" She pulled her library book from her book bag and pretended to read.

"Momma said she's going to call you to babysit soon," he said, exploring his teeth with his tongue for the last bits of candy. "She's joined the Red Cross. Lots of meetings."

"Tell her I'd be glad to." That was only partly true. When they'd first moved in, Billie had enjoyed watching Stanley and his sister. Their bickering was made bearable by the quarters Mrs. Stewart paid. But as soon as Captain Stewart was sent overseas, Doff wouldn't let Billie take a nickel for her time. "The man put his life on the line at D-day," she'd said. "It's your patriotic duty to help out."

Babysitting wasn't as fun after that.

The bus pulled up to the school and Billie gathered her things. "See you later," she said.

"I brought my letter from Poppa for show-and-tell," he said. "Teacher will like it."

"I'm sure she will." Billie smiled.

After calling roll and reading the morning

announcements, Miss Daley invited students to share current events. Emil read from a newspaper clipping about the Battle of Leyte, in the Philippines. "General MacArthur said, um, ah, he would return, um, ah, and he has." When Emil got nervous, he stammered over every other word. It took him forever to read the clipping. Even Miss Daley looked relieved when he finished.

Kit raised her hand as soon as Emil took his seat. "Hazel and I have something to share."

"Please." Miss Daley motioned them up front.

Billie blinked. Not only were they wearing matching sweaters, Hazel's was filled out. It was hard to listen as Kit went on and on about how she and Hazel had spent all day Saturday collecting tinfoil outside the drugstore. "We got a stack about this high!" She demonstrated with her hands. "By the time we add it to our classroom foil ball, it's going to be as big as a watermelon." She nudged Hazel. "Right?"

Hazel nodded, but kept her arms folded across the mountain range of her newly ample chest. She seemed relieved to return to her seat when Kit had finished talking.

It was one thing for Hazel to try to copy Kit's hairstyle. But copying her bosoms? Had she lost her marbles? What was next? Lipstick and rouge? The classroom fell into fuzzy focus until Billie felt a sharp tap on her shoulder.

"Wake up, egghead." Spinner waved a handful of papers in front of Billie's face. Vocabulary assignments. She pulled hers from the stack. Another gold star, even though she was spending more time outside with Bear than inside with Doff's dictionary.

Kit held out her hand on Billie's other side. "The rest of us want our work back, too."

"Sorry." Billie passed them along, shaking the questions about Hazel out of her mind. She smoothed her assignment on her desk, savoring Miss Daley's comment written on the top of the page in her swirly penmanship: "You have a way with words. A pleasure to read!" A warm feeling washed over her.

When the dismissal bell for first recess rang, Billie found herself standing next to Hazel as they shrugged into coats to go outside. It was tight quarters and Billie accidentally caught Hazel with her sleeve.

"Sorry," Billie said. Then she stopped. A scrunched-up wad of toilet tissue lay at Hazel's feet. Billie glanced from the tissue to Hazel's chest. Instead of a mountain range, it was now a single peak.

Kit covered her mouth. "Hazel!" she exclaimed. "You lost your—"

In an instant, Billie knew how to win her friend back. She kicked the tissue under the cubbies before anyone else saw. Then she pushed Hazel's coat at her. "Mayday," she said, signaling with her eyes.

Hazel's forehead wrinkled in puzzlement. Then she glanced down, turning bright red. "Oh my gosh!" She covered herself and made a beeline for the girls' room.

"I told you to use socks!" Kit called after her. She took Clarice's arm. "Did you see what happened?" By the end of recess, the Kit grapevine had done its job.

Hazel sat hunched in her chair when everyone else came back in from recess.

"Are you okay?" Billie asked.

"Just leave me alone." Hazel ducked her head, sniffling.

"But I was only trying to help—"

"I don't need your kind of help." Hazel yanked out her arithmetic book and pretended to study a page on long division.

Billie returned to her own desk.

All she'd done was try to be a friend. What was so wrong with that?

CHAPTER TWELVE

Billie

October 21, 1944

Billie shared peanut butter crackers and her sad story with Bear on the front porch. "Hazel wouldn't even look at me all week." She broke off a chunk of cracker. "Shake." Bear put out his right front paw. "Good boy!" He gobbled down the reward. Teaching Bear to shake had been Tito's idea; now that he had that down, Billie planned to teach "fetch" next. "I bet if you fetched Doff's slippers, she'd let you in the house." She stood, brushing off her dungarees. "Come on. I better tell her we're going."

Even though all Billie heard when she shook her piggy bank was the sorrowful *clink-clink* of two pennies and one lonely nickel, Doff still would not let her accept any money for babysitting for

Mrs. Stewart. Billie hadn't realized it would be so expensive to keep a dog. The few bucks Leo had sent disappeared quickly, even with Mr. Baumann's "family" discount at the Feed and Seed.

Doff sat at the kitchen table, working on the books for the ranch, a stack of mail at her elbow.

"Anything for me?" Billie reached to go through it, hoping for a letter from Leo or Denny.

Doff moved the ledger book, covering the mail. "Just bills." She busied herself with writing down some figures.

"Okay." What was in that stack of envelopes that she didn't want Billie to see?

A quick series of knocks at the back door got Doff's attention. "Oh, there's Mr. Garcia."

When she stepped out to speak to Tito's father, Billie rushed to peek under the ledger. The top envelopes were nothing important, just bills.

The last letter was postmarked San Francisco. Billie's heart skipped a beat. There was no return address, but the handwriting was a lot like the bookplates in the parlor. She turned the envelope over, ready to lift the flap and peek inside.

"Yes, fine. That should do it for today, Mr. Garcia," Doff was saying.

Billie shoved the envelope back where she'd found it.

Doff smoothed her apron as she stepped inside. "That man is a wonder. He got that cranky old tractor running again, with a three-dollar part." She returned to her ledger, burying the letter once again. Billie had lost her chance.

"I'm headed over to Mrs. Stewart's." She fiddled with the corner of the checkered oilcloth on the table, then cleared her throat. "It's been a while since I've bought a war stamp."

"Nope." Doff made an erasure, not even looking up. "You are not to take one penny for watching those kids."

Billie sighed. She grabbed the woven leash Leo had given her, clipped it to Bear's collar, and they headed toward the Stewarts'. The kids loved Bear, so Mrs. Stewart loved Bear, and even allowed him in the house.

After giving Billie some last-minute instructions, Mrs. Stewart left in a cloud of White Shoulders perfume. She wasn't gone five minutes before the grumbling started.

"I want Momma." Didi rubbed her runny nose on MuMu Monkey's head.

"Yeah." Stanley kicked his feet against the chair legs. "You don't make bologna sandwiches right."

"Momma cuts them into triangles," Didi whined. "Ninety-seven triangles."

Billie stepped around Bear to grab a table knife from the silverware drawer. She cut Didi's sandwiches into as many triangles as she could.

"Is that ninety-seven?" Didi glared at the plate suspiciously.

"Yes." Didi couldn't even count to twenty yet.

"Okay." She picked up one of the triangles and took a bite.

"We can play as soon as you two are finished," Billie said. "Do you want triangles, too?"

"Circles," Stanley answered.

Billie tapped the knife against his plate, glancing over at the clock. It'd be at least another whole hour before Mrs. Stewart got back. Billie hoped she'd survive. "Triangles or nothing."

Didi rearranged her sandwich triangles on her plate. "If I have five bites, can we play dollies?"

"I want to play catch-the-cattle-rustlers," Stanley said. "Dolls are for babies."

Billie rubbed her forehead. No wonder Mrs. Stewart had been humming when she left. "Let's find something you both want to play," she said.

"I am not a baby!" Didi stuck her tongue out at her brother.

"Cattle rustlers!" Stanley demanded.

"Dollies!" Didi hollered.

"Rustlers!"

"Dollies!"

Billie waved her hands. "No shouting. We can decide this fairly." She took a toothpick from the container on the table. Out of sight of her charges, she broke it in half. Then she arranged the broken bits of wood in her hand. "You each pick a piece; longest one gets to choose."

Didi picked first. Short straw.

"Ha-ha!" Stanley cheered. "I won. Cattle rustlers!" He ran around the kitchen, waving his toothpick stub. Bear scooted out of his way.

Didi burst into tears. "I don't want to. I always have to be the doggie!" Her head dropped to the table.

Billie moved MuMu Monkey off Didi's plate. "Hey, you're going to get your sandwiches all soggy." That attempt at a joke only made Didi cry harder. Bear tried to hide behind the stove.

Stanley banged into Didi's chair. "Hold up there, Black Bart!"

Billie thought her head might explode from the racket. She stuck her fingers in her mouth and whistled. Bear hopped up and ran to her side. She put on her best Doff I-mean-business voice. "Stanley, sit down and finish your lunch." She got a towel to wipe Didi's tear-sticky face and gave her a sip of water to calm her. "And you finish your lunch, too," she added, but in a gentler tone.

"Why should I?" Didi poked her finger through a piece of bread.

"Well, if you do—" Billie stroked Bear's back, groping for an answer. "If you do, we can have our own Red Cross meeting." She clapped her hands together. "And Bear can be our patient!"

"Can I be a patient, too?" Stanley asked.

"I'm the nurse!" Didi jumped up and down in her chair.

"Lunch first," Billie said.

"My goodness!" Mrs. Stewart exclaimed. "What happened here?"

"We're playing Red Cross." Didi wrapped another rag around Bear's paw.

"Me, too!" Stanley showed off his bandaged arm and leg.

Mrs. Stewart shook her head, a whisper of a smile flicking across her face. Billie realized she hadn't seen Mrs. Stewart smile in a long time. "What a good nurse you are."

"And I'm a good patient, aren't I?" asked Stanley.

"The best." Mrs. Stewart undid the clasp on her handbag and pulled out a coin purse. "Thank you so much."

Billie stepped away. "Oh, no charge."

"You've done enough freebies." Mrs. Stewart pressed some coins into Billie's hand.

"But—" Billie protested.

"I can't ask you to babysit anymore if you don't let me pay." Mrs. Stewart unpinned her hat and set it on the table. "Don't worry. I'll talk to your aunt. Now, let's help our furry patient out of his bandages so he can walk home."

"We don't want Billie to leave," Didi whined.

"Yeah, we were having so much fun," added Stanley. "She makes the best bologna sandwiches."

"Don't worry," Billie said. "I'll come back soon."

"Bear, too!" said Stanley.

Didi waved MuMu Monkey. "Bear, too," she repeated.

"We're a team." Billie reached for her jacket. "Of course he'll come."

As she got close to home, Billie saw Doff heading for the chicken coops. She let Bear off leash and he ran to put his mark on yet another shrub. Billie gunned for the house, up the front porch steps and into the kitchen. She found Doff's paperwork still scattered all over the table. Billie shuffled through the mess, looking for that envelope from San Francisco.

Bear was at the back door, whining. "I know. I know. I'll get your dinner in a second." Billie sifted through the mail. Bill. Bill. Bill. A letter from Doff's best friend in New Mexico. And that was it.

"Hey, Billie!" Doff called from the other side of the back door. "Open up. I've got my arms full." She came in, carrying a foil-covered casserole dish, giving the perfect impression of someone who wasn't trying to hide mail from her great-niece. "Look what Mrs. Garcia made for us! Tamales." She pulled back the foil. "We'll be feasting tonight." Doff got some plates from the cupboard. "Grab the silverware, will you? I didn't eat lunch and I'm starving."

Billie did as she was told. But starving wasn't the only thing Doff was. She was also keeping a secret. What had she done with that envelope? And why was she hiding it from Billie?

CHAPTER THIRTEEN

Denny

October 30, 1944

Something was different. Denny sensed it. Moments later, a lieutenant strode into the room, and eighteen Navajo radiomen hopped to attention. The lieutenant was followed by Sergeants Johnston and Manuelito. Two Anglo Marines brought up the rear, each carrying some kind of machine.

"We've got a little test for you today." Sergeant Johnston waved the new soldiers forward and they set their machines on the desk. "Who knows what these are?"

The Marines had taught them to answer, and promptly. Denny's hand shot up. "A coding machine and a cipher," he answered.

"Right. Lieutenant Hunt here is a signal officer

under General Vandergrift who needs some convincing about our code. Can we provide it?"

Eighteen voices called out, "Sir, yes, sir."

The voices sounded confident, but Denny wondered if any of the others felt thrown back to their school days, as he did. He'd been a kid when he'd been taken from his mother and put with people who could see only skin color, nothing more. Denny remembered the first day at the boarding school. His longing for his family was as powerful as a flash flood, but there was no sympathy for him, or the other Diné children far from home. Before his long black hair was hacked off into the regulation school cut, a matron examined it for lice. She went over his head three times, unwilling to believe he wasn't infested. "They're all filthy," she'd complained to the superintendent. Denny didn't know much English back then, but those words he knew.

This lieutenant also put him in mind of his junior high English teacher. That man had refused to believe Denny could write such an intelligent essay on Jules Verne. When Denny wouldn't confess that he'd plagiarized the essay—because he hadn't—he'd been lashed with a belt. He did everything standing up for the next week.

Denny forced himself to stop remembering. To still the feelings churning inside. He was a Marine. A Marine with an important job to do. *Semper fi*. He took a deep breath; he hadn't realized how loud it was until Jesse gave him a look.

Denny nodded. Focused. Be a Marine.

After a few seconds, his heart rate slowed. And he couldn't help being curious. He'd never seen the Shackle protocol in action, though they'd studied it, along with everything else in the radio operator training. He leaned forward to watch.

"Begay, you and Smith grab a couple of TBYs and get set up in the back of the room. These fellas can work here at the front."

Denny exchanged a look with Jesse. An almost imperceptible nod. "Hut!" Jesse whispered and Denny couldn't help but smile. They'd played football together in high school and beaten some very cocky Anglo teams. Teams that had underestimated them because they were Navajo.

"Hut," Denny whispered back.

Sergeant Johnston turned to Lieutenant Hunt. "Do you want to write the message, sir?" Manuelito handed the lieutenant a pencil and a pad of paper.

Once the coding machine was set up, and the TBY radio turned on, Denny and Jesse slipped on their headphones. Manuelito walked to the back of the room, one copy of the message in hand. Lieutenant Hunt remained at the front, ready to pass the other copy of the message to the code machine operators.

Sergeant Johnston watched the second hand on the wall clock. When it hit the twelve, he barked out, "Go!"

Jesse took the message from Sergeant Manuelito and began to translate. "Arizona, Arizona," he said, announcing that the message to follow was in the Navajo code. He rattled off the time and date, as they'd been trained, then relayed the message, spelling out each letter quickly, clearly, and accurately. He finished with *"Gah, ne-ahs-jah,"* for rabbit, owl. The letters *R* and *O*. Roger and Out.

Denny's hand flew across the pad as he took in each syllable being transmitted. When he finished, he laid down his pencil and handed the pad to Sergeant Manuelito, who delivered it to Lieutenant Hunt.

"Message transmitted and decoded, sir." Manuelito snapped off a salute.

The two Marines working the machines, faces frozen in grim determination, were still encoding their message. Denny felt for them; but like true Marines, they wouldn't quit until the job was done. Finally, Lieutenant Hunt ordered them to stop. They could've been there another hour, trying to send and receive that message.

Lieutenant Hunt shook his head, before shaking Sergeant Johnston's hand. "I guess you've got something there." He left the room without any further comment.

The Anglo radiomen gathered up their gear and headed for the door in Lieutenant Hunt's wake. One of them stopped in the doorway "That was something," he said. "*Semper fi*, buddies. *Semper fi*."

When the door closed behind them, Sergeant Johnston clasped his hands together. "Fine job, men. Fine job." He nodded. "You're ready for action. Which is a good thing. Orders have come in." He crumpled the message that the Anglo radiomen had been working on and tossed it into the waste-basket. "You ship out in a week."

CHAPTER FOURTEEN

|||||||||||||||||||||||||||||||||||||||||||||||||||||||||||||||||||

Billie

November 22, 1944

Billie set a jar of home-canned peaches in the wicker basket sitting on Miss Daley's desk. It felt pretty small compared to Spinner's canned ham. She hurried to tuck it under Emil's donation of a box of crackers.

"Oh, that will be a real treat to the family." Miss Daley smiled. "Thank you, Billie." Of course she said something nice about each student's contribution, even Clarice's one lumpy sweet potato. "I certainly have much to be thankful for with a class as kind as this one." Miss Daley tied a satiny bow to the handle of the basket. "I'll deliver this to the Red Cross office this afternoon. You children are going to make someone's Thanksgiving so much brighter."

As the class filed out for lunch, Spinner elbowed Tito. "Did you bring tamales for the basket?" he asked. "Or beans?" He made a farting sound and Del copied him; they laughed as if they were as funny as Jack Benny.

Tito took his lunch box from his cubby and went to sit by Emil as he usually did. Spinner and Del kept making noises until one of the lunch ladies told them to quiet down or they'd be sent to the principal's office.

Billie found a seat next to Clarice.

"Have you heard from Leo lately?" Clarice popped the lid off her milk bottle. Her sister Charlene had been one of Leo's girlfriends before he fell for Flo.

"A couple of weeks back." Billie unfolded the waxed paper from her sandwich. "He says he got to see Bob Hope when the USO put on a show. And he says he's sick of palm trees."

"He's in the Pacific," Clarice said. "So is the sailor Charlene's going steady with. She knows because they worked out this code before he left."

Billie took a bite of her sandwich. She wished she and Leo had done something like that. The censors were good at blacking out anything that gave a hint about where Leo might be. In his last letter, he'd written that he'd been on a ship for such a long time that when they finally landed on shore, he still felt like he was rocking on the water. The censor had left that part in. "It's going to feel funny not to have him here for Thanksgiving," she said. "Or Christmas."

"If he gets home at all," Clarice added. "Charlene's sailor has lost three best buddies."

Her words knocked the wind out of Billie. She'd stopped reading Doff's newspaper because of the casualties list printed each week. Some nights she could scarcely sleep, terrified that Leo's name might be on it.

Clarice smacked her forehead with the heel of her hand. "Oh. I'm sorry, Billie. I didn't mean— Leo's going to be fine. Think of all those times he got tackled on the football field." She snapped her fingers. "Didn't the coach call him The Tank because nothing could hurt him?"

Billie felt she should say something to make Clarice feel better. But war wasn't a football game.

"I am a dodo brain." Clarice pushed a cookie toward Billie. A peace offering. "Ma's always hollering at me to think before I speak."

"It's okay." Billie pushed the cookie back to Clarice. "I'm not hungry, but thanks." She wrapped her mostly uneaten sandwich back up in the waxed paper. Bear could have it for a snack when she got home. She'd completely lost her appetite.

"And here's around the world." Since his birthday, Tito had been obsessed with his new yo-yo. He let go and it sailed next to his side in a large circle. "I finally figured out that the trick is to throw it hard enough."

Billie nodded, plodding along next to him.

"I was thinking of teaching Bear how to walk the dog," Tito said.

She nodded again.

"You're not even listening, are you?" Tito stopped his hand, palm up, and the yo-yo snapped back into it. "How would a dog be able to yo-yo?"

As if on cue, a black blur barreled toward them. Billie knelt to wrap her arms around Bear. "Bear could."

"With his mouth?" Tito scoffed.

"Oh, I don't know." Billie stood up, shifting her book bag strap back onto her shoulder. Normally, she enjoyed the walk home with Tito. Sometimes he'd teach her about astronomy. Sometimes, a few words in Spanish. But Clarice's words were a jagged sliver, infecting Billie with fear. Sure, Leo was tough. But so was Great-Uncle Hugh. And look what had happened to him.

She scarcely noticed when Tito cut off onto the path that led to his house. Bear nudged her hand with his damp nose. "I have a treat for you today," she said. "A good one. Just don't tell Doff." She broke her sandwich into chunks and fed them to Bear without even asking him to do any tricks. She didn't have the heart for it.

Bear knew to plop down on the porch when they reached the ranch house. "Doff?" Billie called. The kitchen was warm and yeasty. A big metal bowl sat on the kitchen table. Billie lifted the tea towel that covered it, peeking at the small ball of dough. It looked like it still had a couple of hours to rise; when it was ready, the dough ball would nearly fill the bowl. Then she and Doff would shape and bake crescent rolls for the big Thanksgiving feast tomorrow with Flo's family.

A note peeked out from under the bowl. "Gone to town on business. Back for supper. Doff." Billie poured herself a glass of water. What kind of business could Doff have the day before Thanksgiving? She set the empty glass in the sink and headed to her room to change out of her school clothes. When she passed Leo's room, she paused. Then she went inside. She noticed a new framed photo by his bed; Flo, in a dark sweater and a pearl necklace, smiled out at her. Billie crossed over to the closet and opened the door. Leo's sports gear was in a jumble on the floor, as if he'd be back any moment to grab that bat and glove, or that football and helmet. His letterman's jacket hung from a hook on the back side of the closet door. It felt heavy on her shoulders, but a good heavy, like one of Doff's winter quilts, not heavy like worry. Billie tugged the jacket closer around her, the leather sleeves stiff against her arms. In one pocket she found a pack of Black Jack gum. She pulled out a piece. Hard as a rock. She unwrapped it and put it in her mouth anyway. It broke into hard bits, too stale to chew. She sucked as much licorice flavoring out of it as she could.

Bear woofed outside; his signal that someone had driven up. Doff must be home. Billie started to slip off Leo's jacket, then changed her mind. She carried it to her room, hanging it in her own closet. She didn't think Leo would mind her keeping it here. Keeping him close. She spit out the lifeless gum, then patted the jacket as she began to close the closet door. Something crinkled in the opposite pocket.

An envelope. An envelope with a San Francisco postmark. And this one had been opened. She lifted the flap.

"Yoo-hoo!" Doff called. "I'm home."

Billie shoved the envelope back in the pocket to read later. Then she quickly changed into her play clothes and ran out to greet her aunt. Tonight the mystery would be solved!

After the rolls were shaped and baked and stored in the old cracker tin, and after supper, and after she'd settled Bear for the night, Billie finally closed her bedroom door and pulled that envelope out of Leo's letterman jacket pocket. Her heart raced as she lifted the flap.

There was nothing inside.

CHAPTER FIFTEEN

‖‖‖

Billie

"If you're going into town today, we need postage stamps." Billie gathered her school things. "I've got letters to mail for Leo and Denny."

"Me, too." Doff made a note on her shopping list. "Thanks for the reminder. Can you think of anything else?"

An idea had come to Billie as she'd drifted off to sleep. "How about a Seven Up bar?" She fished a nickel out of her coin purse. Yesterday, Hazel had played hopscotch with her. She wasn't about to let that glimmer of hope fade away. Hazel loved Seven Up bars, with seven different kinds of candy in one. It'd be the perfect Christmas and win-back-a-friend gift.

Doff frowned. "Is that your war stamp money?"

"I still have twenty-five cents." Billie opened her coin purse to prove it. "Don't worry, I'm doing my bit today."

"All right, then." Doff took the nickel.

Billie slung her book bag over her shoulder, and Bear accompanied her down the long drive to the Y in the road where Tito met up with them. He was already waiting, reading a magazine and chuckling.

"What's so funny?" Billie asked.

"This joke," Tito answered.

"In *Star and Telescope*?" She picked a burr from Bear's tail.

"Astronomers have funny bones, too," he said indignantly.

Billie tossed the burr away. "Let's hear it."

"So this lady comes up to the astronomy professor after his lecture—"

"You're sure this is a joke?" Billie asked.

Tito gave her a look. "Let me finish."

"I'm listening." She stroked Bear's head. "Both of us are."

"A lady comes up to the astronomy professor after his lecture and says, 'I understand how you measure the distance to the stars, professor. What I don't understand is—" Tito doubled over laughing.

"Is how you learn their names? Learn their names!" he repeated.

Billie forced a smile. "That's a knee slapper, all right." She had read better jokes on Dubble Bubble wrappers, but it seemed mean to say so. She gave Bear a last pat. "Home, boy." He trotted off as the bus pulled up.

Billie spied an empty seat behind Kit and Hazel and quickly slid onto it. "Want to play hopscotch today?" Billie asked hopefully.

Tito kept walking to the back of the bus.

"My dad's store is getting a new shipment of twinsets this weekend." Kit acted as if Billie hadn't spoken. "I'm thinking we should buy baby blue this time." She fluffed her curls. "It sets off my eyes."

"I still haven't paid my parents back for the last one," Hazel said.

"Well, they don't expect you to wear the same sweater over and over, do they?" Kit asked.

A kerfuffle a few seats up prevented Billie from hearing Hazel's answer; she didn't need to. Kit could afford to be a clothes horse because her father managed a department store. But most girls did wear the same dresses and skirts and sweaters over and over to school. And with five kids in her family, Hazel had to make her clothes last even longer than most. She couldn't even count on hand-me-downs, because she was the only girl.

After attendance and the Pledge of Allegiance, Miss Daley pulled out the basket with the war stamp booklets and supplies. "The bad news is that we are lagging behind room 12 in our friendly competition." She smiled brightly. "But it's only December. We still have six months left. I have every confidence that our class will be victorious!" She glanced through the basket. "Oh, I forgot to get the stamps from the office. I'll be right back. Clarice, you are class monitor while I'm gone."

Clarice hopped up, arming herself with a piece of chalk from the blackboard tray, ready to write down the name of any evildoer.

"Well, I'm doing my share to beat room 12." Spinner opened his desk and pulled out a leather coin purse, jingling with change. "My dad gave me money to buy five stamps today."

"How patriotic." Kit fluffed her hair. "I'm buying two."

"Not bad." Spinner leaned across the aisle to flick Billie on the arm. "How about you, egghead?"

Billie edged away from Spinner's fingers. "Miss Daley says it's no one else's business," she said.

"Oh. So your answer is—" Spinner formed his fingers into a circle. "A big fat zero."

"Stop talking, Spinner, or I'm going to write down your name." Clarice held up the long piece of white chalk like a sword.

"Spinner, I'm going to write down your name," Del mimicked.

"And yours, too." Clarice pressed the chalk to the board, ready to write.

"I dare you," Del replied.

Miss Daley tap-tapped back into the room. She glanced at the blank blackboard. "No problems, I see." She beamed at the class. "Thank you, Clarice. Children, give me another moment and I'll be set up for sales."

Spinner hopped out of his seat to be the first in line. "This will be the second book I've filled this year," he bragged. "Another twenty-five-dollar savings bond in the bank. Ka-ching." He pretended to be hitting keys on a cash register.

Miss Daley counted out his stamps. "Every contribution, large and small, makes a difference," she said. "Next?"

"Aren't you coming, Hazel?" Kit called.

Hazel was the only student still seated. She shook her head, cheeks turning pink.

Billie thought of the money in her coin purse. She had enough so that Hazel could buy a stamp, too. Wasn't that what friends did? She stepped out of line. "Here." She set a dime on Hazel's desk. "You don't even have to pay me back."

"Hazel!"

Hazel glanced up as Kit started giggling.

Billie caught Spinner gawking in their direction.

"I don't need charity." Hazel refused to meet Billie's gaze.

Billie snapped her coin purse closed. "I'm trying to be your friend."

Hazel made a shield of her social studies book and ducked behind it. "Stop," she hissed. "Just stop trying."

Spinner moved toward Billie. If he said even one word to her, she didn't know how she'd keep from crying. She tried to ask to go to the nurse, but her words crumpled in on themselves.

"Miss Daley." Tito raised his hand. "It's been a long time since we had a math relay. Could we have one today?"

"Noooo," a few kids groaned.

"Wonderful idea, Tito." Miss Daley looked up from counting money. "I think we can squeeze that in before first recess."

Tito seemed oblivious—last weekend's new word, meaning "unaware"—to the fact that twenty-four sets of eyes were throwing daggers at him. But one set of eyes was not. Billie caught Hazel's look of gratitude. Of course Hazel was grateful. Tito had taken attention away from her.

While Billie had only made things worse.

"Stamps are over there," Doff said. "That candy bar, too. Don't spoil your supper." She nodded toward the far counter while working the bread dough on the table. She'd knead, turn the dough ball a quarter turn, knead, turn, knead, turn. Doff could probably make bread in her sleep.

Billie pasted stamps on her letters to Leo and Denny. "Do you want this?" She held out the Seven Up bar.

"Thanks." Doff placed the dough in a large, greased bowl, turning it over once to get it evenly coated. That way it wouldn't stick while it was rising. "But I don't care for them."

Billie didn't care for Seven Up bars, either. They were Hazel's favorites. "Was there any mail?" Leo owed her a letter.

"In the front hall." Doff washed the flour off her hands. "Mr. Garcia was kind enough to bring it in. I haven't had a chance to look at it yet."

Billie tucked the candy bar in her pocket before flipping through the stack of mail. There *was* a letter from Leo! She was about to tear it open when she noticed another San Francisco postmark in the pile. She set Leo's letter down and glanced over her shoulder. Doff was still puttering in the kitchen. Billie slipped the envelope into her other pocket. "Bear and I are going out to play!" she called. Did her voice sound as guilty as she felt?

But Doff answered the way she always did. "Be back before dark."

Billie whistled for Bear. And they were off.

CHAPTER SIXTEEN

||||||||||||||||||||||||||||||||||||||||||||||||||||||||

Billie

Her feet carried her as if they knew the way. Which they did. She'd been coming to Elephant Rock since she was old enough to wander the ranch by herself. She wanted to get there quickly so she could read the envelope now burning a hole in her pocket, but Bear was determined to sniff each bush and leave his mark on every other shrub. Nose down, he followed trails made by chipmunks or rabbits or blue jays. A warbler sang a complicated song from a nearby tree. Another bird answered back. Billie pounded her feet into the ground harder as she ran. Even birds knew how to make friends. Why couldn't she?

When Bear got out of sight for too long, Billie stuck her fingers in her mouth and whistled. Moments later, he would come loping out from the underbrush, a tangle of tumbleweed stuck on his ear, a burr on his tail, a stick in his mouth. "We haven't got all day!" she complained about the fifth time she had to whistle for him. "Let's go!" She sprinted off, but he quickly overtook her, looping back when he got too far ahead as if to say, *Come on, slowpoke!* By the time Elephant Rock was in sight, he'd run three times as far as she had. Billie paused to catch her breath. "That's where we're going." She pointed to a small trail worn in the rock by years of footsteps. Some hers. But so many others before her. The narrow path left enough room for them to scramble along, side by side, as they climbed. Near the top, Bear nosed past her.

"Okay, okay. So you beat me." She joined him at the top of the elephant's flat head, throwing her arms wide. "Isn't this amazing?"

Between the elephant's "ears" was a smooth dip in the rock; as a kid, she'd pretended that she was a circus rider dressed in satin and sequins, and this spot was her saddle. She'd spent hours waving to imaginary crowds dazzled by her horseback-riding skills. Now it was a lookout post, giving her a clear view of the highway in either direction. Billie settled in, chin on hands, elbows on knees, studying the scene before her. Bear sidled up close.

"This is my favorite view of the valley," she told him. She thought it was even more beautiful than those paintings Miss Daley showed in art appreciation. The gray cord of highway below stitched the orchards and pastures and desert together in a showstopping patchwork quilt of color. Billie had invited Hazel up once to show her. But Hazel hadn't been one for hiking and climbing and getting dirty. She preferred inside activities: tea parties or paper dolls or Monopoly. Last summer, Billie had thought she'd explode if she had to pass Go one more time. Hazel was always the banker, counting out the pretend money as if it were real. "Ten, twenty, thirty." She liked to use the smallest bills possible to make the payout last longer. It made Billie want to jump out of her skin! Now that she thought about it, they always did whatever Hazel wanted. The way she wanted. Even when they went to the show and pooled their money for a treat, Hazel got to pick it out. And she always chose a Seven Up bar. The only part Billie liked was the coconut cream. But that was Hazel's favorite, too, so Billie usually got stuck with maple walnut.

Billie pulled the now-smushed candy bar from her pocket. She unwrapped the gooey mess, unable to tell the difference between the coconut cream and the maple walnut. All it looked like was a complete waste of a nickel.

"I hate maple walnut!" she hollered, pitching that candy bar off the top of Elephant Rock, one piece at a time. About one piece for every year she and Hazel had been friends. And that was the truth of it, she now realized: had been. Had. Been. She crumpled the candy wrapper and shoved it into her pocket. At least she'd never have to eat another lousy Seven Up bar.

A Greyhound bus lumbered along the highway below, heading north. When Billie had first discovered this spot, she would watch every single vehicle rolling past, wondering if it might be the one bringing Dad home. That sedan? That old jalopy? That pickup truck? Maybe he'd found the job he'd gone looking for all those years ago and would tool up in a brand-new two-tone coupe. Well, newish, since all metal was going to guns and tanks and other military equipment because of the war. The Greyhound's wheels rolled rough against the pavement, scraping out a rhythm: *don't forget—don't forget—don't forget.*

She leaned back. That's why she'd given this rock its name. Because elephants didn't forget. But people sure did. They forgot appointments. They forgot about old friends. Forgot about their own kids. The truth was, it was getting harder all the time for Billie herself to remember. Was Dad a redhead or had she imagined that detail? And was his laugh like air blowing music over the mouths of empty Nehi bottles? Did he smell of Black Jack gum and Barbasol? No, that was Leo. For such a long time now, she had believed that, one day, she wouldn't have to remember anymore. That their father would drive down this highway and right back into their lives. Not forever. Just long enough for her to ask him a question. One question.

She hadn't realized she was shivering until she pulled the envelope from her pocket. After all the years of wondering how and when Dad might return, the answer might be right here, in her hands. Bear shifted to sniff the envelope. "It's not for you." She moved it out of reach. It wasn't really for *her*, either, being addressed to Doff.

She squirmed a little.

But. The handwriting was so like Dad's.

Could Billie peel the seal open without Doff noticing? She gently tugged at the pointed end of the flap. A crumb of paper tore off. She tried to press it back on, but it wouldn't stick. Maybe Doff would think it got torn at the post office.

Billie's heart pounded.

She couldn't do it.

Not even for a letter from her father.

She stood up, brushing sand from the seat of her dungarees. "Come on, Bear." She started heading down the trail. "We've got to put this back."

"I was surprised you didn't read that letter from Leo right away," Doff said as they sat down to eat.

Billie gulped. "Well—" She took a sip of milk. "I was saving it for dessert." She smiled brightly.

Doff nodded. "That's a good idea. Make 'em last." She passed Billie a serving dish.

Breathing easier, Billie ate her supper. It seemed like Doff hadn't noticed the San Francisco letter had gone missing and reappeared. She hopped up from the dinner table when they'd finished. "Let me clean up," she said.

Doff looked at her.

"Really." Billie shooed her aunt out of the kitchen and into the parlor. "Listen to one of your radio shows." She turned on the radio and brought over the footstool.

Doff settled in.

On her way back to the kitchen, Billie quickly went through the mail on the table in the hall. She plucked Leo's letter from the stack and put it in her pocket. She shuffled through the rest of the envelopes. The letter from San Francisco was gone. When had Doff picked it up? Where had she taken it? And why didn't she want Billie to see it?

After Billie did the dishes, she got Bear settled on the sun porch for the night, then headed for her room.

"What did Leo have to say?" Doff asked.

Billie pulled the letter from her pocket. "Haven't read it yet. I'll let you know at breakfast."

She grabbed Leo's letterman jacket and tugged it over her shoulders before flopping on her bed. Her brother's letter rested against her upraised knees. *"Dear Billie, You're right. I can't tell you where I am. I keep expecting to bump into Denny, though. Stranger things have happened! One guy in my platoon met up with his cousin on—"* She couldn't read the next word because the censor had scribbled over it. *"Isn't that a kick in the pants? Glad to hear that Mr. Garcia is working out so well. That means I'll probably be out of a job when I get out of the service! (Ha-ha.) Seriously, I've been thinking about trying to go to college after all this. Don't faint. It's just that I'm seeing there's a big world out here. And I'd like to be part of it. Gotta sign off, squirt. Don't let the bedbugs bite. Love, Leo. PS I keep forgetting to tell you—I didn't get you a leash for Bear."*

Billie puzzled over Leo's PS. If he hadn't given her the leash, who had? Doff? That didn't make sense. Maybe it had been Denny. That was probably it. She'd ask him about it the next time she wrote.

Now her eyes went back to the top of the page and she reread Leo's letter. He sure could pack a lot of news in a short space. College! That would be something, considering he'd never done a lick of homework unless Doff hounded him. Maybe being in the Marines had changed him. Hopefully not too much. Doff seemed pretty sold on Leo taking over the ranch someday. Billie best not say anything about the college thing. That was Leo's place. Besides, if Doff could keep secrets, so could Billie.

She pulled out some paper and the Parker Vacumatic pen. *"Dear Leo: Got your letter; thanks. We haven't seen much of Flo since Thanksgiving. Her job at the Richmond Shipyards keeps her pretty busy. That would be something if you ran into Denny. I've written him a few letters but haven't heard anything since he let us know he got our holiday care package. He said the book we sent was exactly what he wanted!"* She paused to refill the pen with ink. What would Leo say about the mysterious letters from San Francisco? Would he think they were from Dad, too? Or would he just say Billie had been watching too many movies? She decided to hold off on writing about them, but she was reluctant to put down the pen. When she was writing, it was as if she was talking to her brother. As if he weren't far, far away. It wasn't like his being away at boot camp. Then, she only had to miss him for six weeks. She snugged the jacket tight around her, breathing hard and deep of the fading scents of Black Jack and Barbasol.

A lonely coyote howled in the distance. Billie knew how he felt. She felt a bit like howling herself. She blinked hard to keep Clarice's words from creeping back in.

The coyote howled again. Then from the sun porch, Bear answered, reminding Billie that she might not have two-legged friends, but she had a faithful four-legged one. She pressed the pen nib to the paper once more.

"Bear still walks with me to the bus each morning. Tito meets us about halfway. Sometimes he brings me one of his abuelita's warm tortillas. He likes to talk. Mostly about the stars. Sometimes it's like listening to the encyclopedia. But he got me to thinking that no matter where you are or how far apart we are, we both look at the same moon each night. Watch out for bedbugs and write back soon! Love, Billie."

She blotted the letter and folded it into an envelope, ready for a stamp in the morning. Teeth brushed and in her nightie, she pulled back the curtains at her window. There it was. She placed her hand on the glass, as if touching the moon's face. "I'm here, Leo," she whispered.

No one answered back.

CHAPTER SEVENTEEN

Denny

December 20, 1944

The guy climbing into the hammock above his woke Denny up. Once awake, it was impossible to go back to sleep. Not with three tiers of hammocks fit together like matchsticks in a box. Too many sweaty bodies; too many seasick Marines using their helmets for basins; too many other smells Denny didn't even want to think about.

He rolled out of bed and headed for the deck. The ship's pitching and hawing didn't help his stomach much, but at least he'd managed to keep his motion sickness pills down. Jesse had been puking since they'd boarded. Denny wouldn't take anything for seasickness tonight, though; the phenobarbital made him sleepy.

At the rail, he gulped for fresh air, tugging at the

khaki shirt clinging to him as if fresh out of his mother's washtub. Nothing ever got dry in the tropics.

A large gull overhead caught his attention: It kited up and around, bright white against a dishwater predawn sky. The movement quickly unsettled his already wobbling stomach, so Denny lowered his gaze to the watery horizon. Dotted with hundreds of ships like theirs, it stretched as far as he could see. Growing up in the desert, he'd had no way to imagine this much water in the world.

The ship dipped and his stomach again threatened to rebel. Denny gripped the rail tighter, gritted his teeth. He'd found if he stared at the sea long enough, hard enough, the endless blue would give way to the apricot-colored sand surrounding his mother's hogan, and then up would sprout sage-green piñon pines, bladed yucca plants tipped with white blossoms, and the soft silver foliage of rabbit-brush. After a time, the bobbing white bits of foam turned into lambs and sheep and goats. Denny glued his eyes to the scene, barely blinking, counting heads in his watery flock.

Sometimes, if he stood there long enough, the

faint tinkling of lambs' bells would reach his ears. And he could forget he was on a ship made miniature by an enormous ocean. He could forget about his nausea, and the dreadful stink belowdecks.

He could almost forget he was about to go to war.

CHAPTER EIGHTEEN

Billie

Billie knew that if she said something, Doff would go right to school and straighten Miss Daley out. But once a teacher had been straightened out by Doff, they never seemed as happy to see Billie again.

So Billie had kept quiet for a week and now it was January 17. Every fifth grader boarding the bus was loaded down with father-related paraphernalia, eager to participate in Miss Daley's assignment. Their teacher had decided that, since school dismissed before Father's Day on June 17, the class would celebrate the holiday in January. Unlike her classmates, Billie had nothing under her arm. Nothing in her book bag.

After lunch, Miss Daley kicked off the festivities by holding up a photograph of her own father, decked out in some kind of fancy uniform. "Papa volunteered in World War I, flying with the Lafayette Escadrille. He flew a Voisin biplane." She explained that the squadron was composed of American volunteers, who signed up as early as 1915. "After the war, he came home and opened a newspaper in our town." She displayed the photo on her desk, then took a seat. "I cannot wait to learn more about your fathers," she said. "Who would like to go first? Emil?"

Emil held up several carved wooden lasts, forms that his father used to make shoes for everyone in Emil's family. "He is the third generation of cobblers," Emil said. "Papa learned from his grandfather in Sweden."

"Are you learning the craft, too?" Miss Daley asked.

Emil stammered. "Yes, ma'am. It is our way."

When he finished, Hazel made her way to the front; the photo album tucked under her arm was one Billie had seen countless times while playing at Hazel's house. Hazel slowly flipped through the pages, showing the black-and-white mementos of her father's foray into show business with an act called Joe French and the Frenchettes. "He tried to teach us kids his old soft-shoe routine, but we all seem to have two left feet."

Billie remembered getting dance lessons from Mr. French. Like Hazel, she couldn't get the hang of it either, but Mr. French was wonderful. She wished she could've seen him on the vaudeville stage.

When the applause died down, Miss Daley looked at her grade book. "Who would like to go next? Spinner?"

"I don't think Billie's had a chance yet," Spinner said. "I'm sure she'd like a turn."

Kit giggled, but Hazel had the courtesy to turn chalk white.

Billie couldn't think what to say or do.

Tito popped up. "May I please go next, Miss Daley?" He held a small paper sack.

"Of course." She waved him to the front of the room.

Tito adjusted his glasses on his nose before

speaking. "My family is from Jalisco, from a long line of vaqueros, which are Mexican cowboys. It was said that my great-grandfather dismounted his horse only to dance with a pretty girl."

While the boys groaned and the girls giggled, Tito opened his sack. "The vaqueros had to learn to braid rawhide to make the reata. Like this." He pulled out a long rope.

"That's a work of art," Miss Daley commented. "Beautiful."

"We don't have cows now. Horses either. But my father still taught me how to make the reata. I made a piece for each of you." He moved around the room. Billie got a jolt when he placed a short length of braided rawhide on her desk.

It was just like Bear's woven leash. She worried at the bit of rawhide, turning it over and over. It was too similar to be a coincidence.

"Thank you, Tito." Miss Daley put her reata next to her father's photograph. "Or perhaps I should say *gracias*."

Tito's ears pinked as he sat down.

"Oh, dear. Look at the time." Miss Daley fussed

at her hair. "We'll have to finish these wonderful presentations tomorrow."

As the final bell sounded, Billie gathered her things and headed for the bus. One more day and this celebration of fathers would be behind her. She slid into the first available empty row. As Tito walked down the aisle, he paused. "Is that seat free?" he asked.

Billie nearly said no out of habit. Then she slid over to the window. "Yes. Yes. Please sit down." Before he'd even gotten settled, she blurted out, "The leash was from you, wasn't it?"

His brown eyes lit up behind his glasses. "You didn't have enough money and I had plenty of rawhide." He shrugged. "It wasn't as fancy as the ones from the store."

"It was really nice of you," Billie said. "Really nice."

Spinner and Del swaggered onto the bus and plunked themselves down right behind them.

"Hey, Tito," Spinner pushed into their conversation. "Where did you say you came from again? Nabisco?"

"You heard me." Tito opened up his constellation book. "Jalisco."

"Oh, that's right." Spinner reached across and slapped the book out of Tito's hands. "Where did your grandfather get a horse anyway? Steal it?"

"Knock it off, Spinner." Billie bit off each word.

Tito picked up his book. Smoothed a bent page.

"Cat got your tongue?" Spinner flicked Tito's ear. Del laughed.

Tito didn't even flinch. He casually turned another page, doing a great imitation of being engrossed in his book.

"Oh, who cares about some old Mexican?" Del asked.

"You said it." Spinner tugged on Billie's pigtail. "Why didn't you make a presentation today?"

Tito tapped Billie's leg with his book. She understood the message. *Ignore them.* That's what he'd done and they were leaving him alone. For now.

"What do you think, Del?" Spinner leaned farther forward. "Shouldn't everyone have a chance to talk about their dad?"

"Absotootly," Del said.

The bus slowed. It wasn't his stop, but Spinner got up. "If I were your dad, I would've walked out, too," he said.

A firecracker exploded inside Billie's brain. "Don't." The word came out strangled.

"What?" Spinner held up his hands, acting all innocent.

"Don't you. Ever. Talk about my father again." Her hands clenched into fists.

"Let it go, Billie." Tito pushed her back onto the seat.

Spinner leaned in. She could smell the tuna fish he'd had for lunch. "Probably took one look at you and hit the road."

Billie jumped off her seat and grabbed Spinner's shirt. "Not another word."

"You're right." Spinner smirked. "Why waste my breath on that loser?"

Something snapped. Billie brought her arm down. Hard. Brought Spinner's head down hard. Against the seat back.

"My nose!" he screeched. Blood spurted. "My nose!"

"Mr. Jones!" Kit called out. "Spinner's hurt."

Tito tugged Billie out of the seat and down the aisle.

"This isn't our stop," she said.

"It is today." He pushed her into the stairwell and off the bus.

CHAPTER NINETEEN

Billie

They stood by the side of the highway as the bus pulled away.

Billie's legs were cooked spaghetti noodles.

"I hope you know your way home from here." Tito pushed his glasses up his nose. "Because I sure don't."

"I need to sit down." Billie wobbled over to a rock.

"What were you thinking?" Tito asked.

She stared at the ground. "I wasn't." Tears dripped onto the skirt of her dress.

Tito passed her a handkerchief. "Spinner couldn't even *spell* lout," he said.

Billie wiped her eyes, sniffling. "He's a brute and a barbarian. And has bananas for brains."

"That's the spirit." Tito perched on a rock nearby, smiling.

She managed a smile in return.

His face turned serious. "You are a thousand times smarter than he is. Why do you even pay attention to him?"

"Didn't you hear what he said?" Billie crumpled the handkerchief into a soggy ball.

"I've heard plenty worse." Tito shuffled his feet in the dirt. "When you're Mexican, you can run into a lot of Spinners."

Billie thought about Kit's rude comment that day in the Feed and Seed. "That's crummy."

Tito tilted his head back, studying the sky. "Do you know Pluto was discovered only about a dozen years ago? And that there might be other planets up there that we don't know about yet?"

Billie shielded her eyes, looking skyward as well. "I bet you'll find one," she said.

"I think I could," he said. "I really think I could. But not if I listen to people like Spinner."

Billie was quiet for a moment. "He shouldn't have said what he did about my dad."

"Nope, he shouldn't." Tito nodded in agreement. "Henry Ford said not to find fault but find a remedy."

Billie made a face. "I'm guessing giving someone a bloody nose is not the kind of remedy he had in mind."

"I kind of doubt it."

"Well, I guess I'd better get home and face the music." Billie stood, brushing off the back of her skirt.

"Do we go this way?" Tito pointed.

"For an astronomer, you have a terrible sense of direction." She felt lighter despite the fact she'd get read the riot act when she got home. "This way."

"Go ahead." Billie folded her arms across her chest. "Don't even ask for my side of the story." The news had beat her home.

"It doesn't matter." Doff settled heavily in her reading chair. "Giving someone a bloody nose is never excusable." She pressed her fingers to her mouth. "It could be broken." Shook her head. "Good heavens, Billie. His dad owns half this darned county."

Billie swallowed hard, furious at the fact that her lip was quivering. Why try to explain things?

Doff wouldn't care. Didn't care. The lump in her throat grew harder as Billie remembered the few times Leo had come home after a scuffle at school. "Boys will be boys," Doff would say. She left no doubt that she approved of Leo's actions. And pretty much completely disapproved of Billie's.

"Can I go now?" Billie asked.

Doff exhaled vigorously but didn't say anything.

Billie got up, intending to go to her room. That's where she'd probably be spending a lot of time in the near future.

"Sit." Doff motioned the chair opposite.

Billie stopped in the doorway. It was the last thing she wanted to do, but she obeyed. Slumped in the chair, she ducked her head so she'd be out of view of her parents' wedding photograph. The parlor mantel clock *tick-tick-ticked*. From the kitchen, the percolator sighed. Doff's rough hand *scritch-scratched* as it rubbed back and forth, back and forth on her flowered apron.

"So what is it?" Doff finally broke the silence.

Billie shook her head, confused.

"Your side of the story." Doff sat back. "What is it?"

Billie reached out for Bear, but he was on the sun porch. If only she could feel his warm fur under her hand to give her courage. "Today was Father's Day in January at school," she began. "A big celebration."

Doff's hand went to her forehead. "Great Scott. Why didn't you say something?"

"I like Miss Daley." Billie tugged her dress hem over her knees. "She didn't mean anything by it."

"All right, then." Doff drummed her fingers on the end table. "Where does Spinner fit in?"

Billie took a deep breath and then out rushed everything Spinner had said on the bus. "I know I shouldn't have grabbed him," she said. "But I had to make him stop."

"By bloodying his nose?"

"That was an accident. I didn't mean to hurt him. I really didn't. But when he said those things—"

"Sticks and stones can break my bones, but words can never hurt me," Doff recited, but with a question mark at the end.

"But words do hurt." Billie wiped at the tear that had betrayed her. "Especially when they're true."

"You have a point there." Doff tipped her head back. "It's hard to explain to those who weren't there. The Depression was a dream killer. Not a job to be found. Bankers lined up with janitors at soup kitchens. My own lawyer peddled apples on San Francisco street corners. I had to sell off my cattle, my horses." She pressed her fingers to her eyes. "Some of the stock, I just turned loose. Hoped for the best. It was an ugly, ugly time."

Doff had never looked so old. So sad. She slipped her hands in her apron pockets. "Your dad brought you kids here, and did his best around the ranch. But he hated weeding and hoeing. Hated the quiet nights. He especially hated my chickens." She gave a rueful chuckle. "Such a city boy. Give him those bright lights and the hustle-bustle." Her gaze rested on Billie's parents' wedding photo. "Spinner is right. Your father did leave."

"I didn't mean *that* was the true part." Billie stared at her shoes as she whispered the next words. "The true part was that he left because of me."

Doff was across the room in a flash, kneeling in front of her. "Is that what you believe?"

Billie couldn't answer.

"Look at me." Doff took her hands. "I am not going to make up some cockamamie story about *why* your father left, just to make you feel better."

Billie tried to pull away. Why couldn't Doff be soft, just once?

"That came out wrong. What I mean is that no one can really know why a person does such and so." She closed her eyes briefly, as if in prayer. "You know how I've been letting out the hems of your school dresses? No matter how clever a seamstress I am, there will come a point when there'll be nothing left to turn under." Doff squeezed Billie's hands. "I think your father's pride had been let out as far as it could go."

"But we're family!" Billie threw the words at Doff. "If he loved us, he should've taken us with him! Not left us here."

"Oh, my knees." Doff creaked to a stand, balancing herself on the arm of Billie's chair. "And what would he have taken you to? A hobo camp? A ratty tenement? The world out there was cruel enough to a man on his own. There would be nothing for a man with two children. Nothing." She pressed her lips together. "The truth is your father loved you so much that he left you. Here. Where you'd be safe. And fed." Doff stroked Billie's hair. "And loved." She bent to kiss the top of her head, the first kiss Billie could remember. That tenderness stiffened Billie's resolve.

"Has he been writing you?" She stared at her great-aunt. "Dad, I mean."

Doff took a step back. "What on earth gave you that idea?" Her face wrinkled in genuine puzzlement.

"I saw some letters." Billie tipped her head side to side. "It looked like his handwriting."

Doff blinked. Thinking.

"From San Francisco," Billie added.

"Oh." She pursed her lips. "I hadn't planned to talk to you about that yet." Doff smoothed a gray hair back into place. "I can read between the lines of Leo's letters. As they say, it's going to be hard to keep him down on the farm after he's seen Paree." She smiled. "Though we don't know that he's seen Paris. Maybe Honolulu. The point is, he's getting a taste of that big wide world. And I honestly wouldn't blame him for seeking his fortune elsewhere." Her features were edged in sorrow, despite her light tone. "And you'll be wanting to spread your wings, too. So I've been making arrangements to sell the ranch to Mr. Garcia. Those letters are from my lawyer."

"Not from Dad?" After a fleeting sting of disappointment, Billie realized she'd known it all along. Why on earth would her father have gotten in contact after all these years? So many feelings kaleidoscoped through her heart: sadness, relief, hope. Sadness that the letters weren't from Dad. Relief at letting go of a huge burden. Hope for whatever came next.

"I'm sorry, Billie." Doff patted her hand. "I'm sure I've done a lot of it wrong, never having had children myself, but I wouldn't have traded a second with you and Leo for anything." She moved toward the kitchen. "That was a lot of soap opera for one afternoon," she said. "Some Ovaltine might be just the ticket."

Billie sat for a moment longer in the parlor. It was funny how one word could make such a difference. Sure, Spinner was right: Her father *had* left her. But Doff was right, too: Dad had left her *here*. He hadn't left her because he didn't love her; he left her because he did.

She was going to have to sit with that idea for some time, but Billie was beginning to think that love was bigger than any dictionary definition.

CHAPTER TWENTY

Billie

February 7, 1945

Dear Leo,

Doff says to quit bugging you but just how much time does it take to write a gosh-darn letter anyway? I have read your last one so many times, it's practically dandelion fluff. Even a postcard would be fine!

Tito's baby sister Isabella turns three this weekend. The Garcias invited us to a fiesta to celebrate. I couldn't believe Doff said yes! Mr. Garcia is probably the only person in this whole county who doesn't make Doff blow her top every other day. You know how she is about her chickens. Mr. Garcia said she should feed them broccoli. And she did it! I know your jaw is probably on the floor. Anyway, that's how much she listens to him. I haven't said anything to her, don't worry, but

I think you shouldn't lose sleep over your plans to go to college.

Flo wrote that she might make it home for her mother's birthday, which is March 18 in case you want to send a birthday letter. Probably not a bad idea to butter up your future mother-in-law! (Har, har.) And Flo says I can wear any color dress I want for the wedding, even though Doff thinks I should wear pink. Blech.

Okay, I have to sign off so I can get to school. Bear says, "Woof!" If you do happen to run into Denny out there wherever you are, tell him he owes me a letter, too.
Don't let the bedbugs bite,
Love, Billie

"Who has the pinking shears?" Kit called out above the buzz of twenty-four students hard at work.

"Me. Just a sec." Clarice finished cutting out a heart and handed the shears to Kit.

"The soldier that gets yours will be so lucky," Hazel told Kit.

Billie glanced at Kit's handiwork. The white lace edging was nice, but the card wasn't anything to fawn over. She'd discovered that word in Doff's dictionary over the weekend when she'd looked up how to spell *fiesta*.

"I can't picture a Marine wanting something frilly and pink." Emil drew a waxy white stripe across a blue construction paper heart. "I'm making mine red, white, and blue."

"Me, too!" Spinner grabbed a piece of blue paper.

"Me three," added Del. Soon all the boys in the class were making Valentine cards with a patriotic theme.

Billie pasted another gold star on the frilly red heart she'd cut out. Would a homemade Valentine really cheer up an injured soldier?

"I wish we could go with Miss Daley and help hand out the cards," Kit said.

Hazel agreed. "Mom's Red Cross ladies go every week to Camp Pendleton to deliver mail at the hospital. She says the soldiers are so glad to get it."

"Too bad we aren't fourteen," Clarice chimed in. "Then we could go, too."

Billie was relieved about the hospital's rule against visitors under fourteen. It wasn't that she was squeamish about seeing injuries. Much. But she knew if she stepped one foot into that place, she'd be reminded that Leo or Denny could easily be one of those recovering from war wounds. She'd lost enough sleep over them as it was. It didn't help that she hadn't heard from Denny since New Year's. And Leo's last letter had arrived at the end of January. For once, she regretted having a vivid imagination. It was too easy to think about what might be keeping them from writing.

"Do you like it?" Tito showed off the card he'd made. On the back of the white heart, he'd drawn a red cross and the words *Todos esperamos que te mejores pronto.*

"Pronto?" Billie read. "Does that mean fast?"

Tito nodded. "It says, 'We all hope you get well soon.'" He added a flourish to the border. "I figure there have to be some Mexican-American soldiers, too, right?"

"Right." Billie went back to working on her card.

Spinner passed Tito's desk on his way to the pencil sharpener. "What does that say?"

"We all hope you get well soon," Billie jumped in. "I think it's nice."

"You would." Spinner sharpened his pencil. When he returned to his desk, he raised his hand.

Miss Daley called on him. "Yes, Spinner?"

"These cards are going to Americans," he said. "They should be in American."

"I think you mean English," Miss Daley corrected. "But I'm a little confused."

"Look." Spinner pointed at Tito's card.

Prickles of anger crept up Billie's legs, into her gut. They were all having a nice time, pitching in for the war effort. Doing something good for the fighting men. Why did Spinner have to ruin things?

"My Spanish is terrible." Miss Daley smiled. "Can you read it for me?"

Tito did.

"What a lovely sentiment." Miss Daley looked thoughtful as she walked to the front of the room, drawing the students' attention with her. "You know, I went to the movies last weekend."

"Me, too," Del blurted out. "*Arsenic and Old Lace*, right? It was a riot."

Miss Daley nodded. "It certainly had many humorous moments. And I do love Cary Grant's accent." She rested against the desk as she looked out the window. "The reason I brought it up is because of the newsreel I saw between the shows. Do you remember that, Del?"

"He was out buying more Raisinets," Spinner said.

Del blushed. "I was hungry, okay?"

"Well, what you missed was a newsreel featuring clips of the faces of the war. The camera panned over all kinds of men in uniform and I was struck by the fact that there were white faces, brown faces, black faces. Even the faces of men of Japanese heritage."

Miss Daley patted her heart, as if getting ready to say the Pledge of Allegiance. She continued. "All those men. Together. Fighting for our country. For a good cause." She pushed away from her desk. "It reminded me that, here in America, we may all come from different places. May even speak different languages. But when push comes to shove and a wrong needs righting, we roll up our sleeves and pitch in. When I saw that newsreel, I thought to myself that this country is perfectly named: the *United* States."

Billie could see twenty-four heads bobbing in agreement around her. Even Spinner's.

Miss Daley picked up a piece of chalk. "And that is enough of a lecture for today. Billie, will you collect the completed cards? And while the rest of you clean up the paper and scissors and glue, I'll write next week's spelling words on the board."

Tito seemed to stand a bit taller as he added his finished card to the growing stack in Billie's hands.

"*Gracias,*" she said.

He grinned. "You're welcome."

CHAPTER TWENTY-ONE

Denny

February 19, 1945

Denny glanced through the supplies he'd been handed: a dented mess kit, extra pairs of socks, some K-rations, and a bar of Fels-Naphtha. Just looking at that bar of soap made saliva rush to his mouth. He shoved it deep in his duffel. Then he opened the K-rations, removing the smokes to trade for gum. And stamps. He owed Billie a letter. More than one.

It was quiet belowdecks. The men were all up top, staring over the gunwales, pinned down by the heavy weight of anticipation. Some sat on their haunches, using their thighs as desks to write letters home; others talked in quiet knots. The padre weaved his way around the deck, giving blessings, saying prayers. He made the sign of the cross on a kid who looked like he was about to lose his lunch.

This was nothing like communications school, where they'd sat in neat rows, memorizing code. The barracks had been cool, the food hot, and the creases in each Marine's trousers sharp enough to slice bread. The men on this deck were sweaty and rumpled, and food was the farthest thing from anyone's mind.

Denny spent half the night wondering what the fighting would be like. And half the night trying not to think about it. Whatever lay ahead, he bet it'd be nothing like the John Wayne movie shown on the ship a few nights back, where only the bad guys died. The casualty lists in the papers proved that wasn't true.

One of *cheii*'s friends had fought in the First World War and Denny had once asked him to talk about his experience. "These are not stories for young men," the man said. "I don't want one word from my mouth to glorify war." Grandfather's friend had shaken his white head solemnly. "There is nothing noble about killing."

Denny tried to keep his mind on the things that made him happy—his mother, pistachio ice cream,

Bear—but fearsome thoughts fought to take charge. He paced back and forth until he ran into a bunch of guys who planned to stay up all night, playing poker.

Denny watched, too jittery to sleep. Willis got a good hand and wanted to raise but was out of chips, so Denny spotted him three of his K-ration smokes. Willis ended up getting beat by a straight flush.

"I owe you, pal." He yawned.

"Forget it." Denny crouched, his back to the gunwales, and tipped his helmet over his head. "I'm going to get some shut-eye," he lied. Sleep was impossible. A few hours later, at dawn, there was Jesse on deck, reciting his prayers, touching corn pollen to his head and tongue.

Denny couldn't help finishing the prayer along with Jesse: "In beauty all is made whole. In beauty all is restored."

Jesse bent to pick up his helmet, his eye catching Denny's. There was a question in it, one he would never ask aloud. Which was good because Denny wasn't sure how to answer it. Had he turned his back on his culture? It probably seemed so to Jesse. When was the last time Denny had prayed? Had opened the buckskin bag at his neck to offer a pinch of the sacred corn pollen to the rising sun?

If *cheii* could see him now, he would surely think Denny had set aside the Navajo way. He shook himself. All he wanted right now was to be a good Marine. That was what would save him. Would bring him home. Not corn pollen prayers.

"Come on, men, let's go." The sergeant signaled that it was time to climb over the gunwales, scramble down the ropes and onto the LCVPs, the flat-bottomed boats that ferried men and equipment to the beaches.

Denny tightened his helmet and followed orders.

CHAPTER TWENTY-TWO

Bear

His sleeping space felt confining. The dog paced forth and back, forth and back. Was it a full moon, calling him to remember his wild past? Or was something else calling to him?

He turned his big head toward the opening behind him. Every morning, his girl walked through that opening. Bringing food. Love. That was a direction his head—and heart—would most often turn.

But something outside pulled at him. This was no coyote call. No sneaky raccoon after poultry. It was a sound he had not heard before. And yet was as familiar as his own four paws. It carried a reminder of a friendly greeting. Of kind hands wrapping bruised ribs.

But this sound was a plea.

A cry for help.

A prayer.

The dog paced.

Soon, he must answer that call.

CHAPTER TWENTY-THREE

Denny

February 19, 1945

The first wave reached shore without incident. The second wave, too.

"Man, we must really have Tojo on the run," someone behind Denny observed. "Don't look like there are any Japanese left on this stinking island."

Denny hoped the man's words were true.

He and Jesse were part of the third wave. Their Higgins boat, that reliable old LCVP, bounced like a toy as they headed for the island. Iwo Jima. In the briefings, they'd been told it was four and a half miles long, and two and a half miles wide, at most. They hadn't been told how bare and dead it looked. Not one tree in sight. Hillocks of dirt or sand dotted the flats like brown blisters; at the southern end of the island, Mount Suribachi rose up like a clenched fist.

The boat ride took three minutes. "Everybody out!" the coxswain hollered.

Denny went over the side and was immediately underwater. Gasping and spitting, he bobbed back up, lifting his arms above the waves to keep his gun and radio dry. The current shoved him backward, toward the boat. And the water was too deep to touch bottom. The only way to move forward was to wriggle like an eel. After an eternity he reached the beach, but that proved no relief. His eyes burned from the sulfur smell of rotten eggs. The coarse volcanic ash grabbed at his boots, pulling them deep, making it nearly impossible to walk. A hundred yards away, a jeep sat, out of commission, buried to its hubcaps, unable to gain traction in the loose terrain. Denny was exhausted and he hadn't even reached the command outpost yet.

"This is like walking through marbles." Jesse struggled next to him. "At least we don't have to be in a hurry." He glanced around, a puzzled expression on his face. "I thought they'd be hitting us with everything they had."

At the briefings, they'd been told there could be thousands of Japanese on the island, and that they'd dug themselves in, using the natural caves of the island as well as pillboxes for protection. They'd also built a series of tunnels.

"Maybe they saw us coming and pulled out," Denny said, though he didn't believe it. Not from what he'd heard about the Japanese. They'd rather die than give up.

The peace and quiet lasted for about one hour.

Then chaos shredded the calm into bits.

The enemy pummeled them with the works: guns, mortars, and grenades. Dense smoke rolled over them like bulldozers; Denny fought to keep Jesse in sight. And the noise. It was as if every evil thing in the universe had lifted its voice in a terrible concert of screeching and keening and moaning. The din wormed its way into Denny's marrow; he wondered if he'd ever be free of it.

He endured the next hours of his life by sending his heart home, recalling the quiet times spent herding his mother's flock to the summer pasture.

That way, he could look past the bodies bobbing in the surf, the screams of "Medic, medic!," the snick of a sniper's bullet brushing his uniform sleeve.

When he and Jesse finally reached their assigned position, the commander didn't know what to do with them. "You've got guns, use 'em," he bellowed. So they stumbled along with the other soldiers—one step forward and two back on that slippery rock—shooting, running, shooting. And diving behind any cover they could find.

Their small platoon grew smaller. Denny tried not to think about the dead or their ghosts. He focused every ounce of his being on doing his duty. On being a Marine.

Their immediate goal was a notch beyond a nearby fold in the earth, high enough that they couldn't see over it. Couldn't see what waited on the other side.

Drenched in sweat and panting like dogs, the men crawled on their stomachs. His elbows raw and bleeding, Denny followed two Marines he didn't know.

He didn't flinch at the explosion. But he turned to see if Jesse was still behind him.

Check.

He turned his gaze forward again.

The Marines he'd been following were gone. Completely gone.

"You two!" the CO screamed at some guys to Denny's left. "Take their place."

As ordered, the Marines scrambled into position.

They, too, were killed.

"That machine gun's got us pinned down," Manuelito yelled. "We're trapped."

Denny's head dropped to the ground, the sand abrading his forehead; blood dripped onto his closed eyelids.

He should have said his prayers this morning.

It looked like this was the end.

|||||||||||||||||||||||||||||||||||||||||||||||||||||||||||||||||||||||||||||||||||||

CHAPTER TWENTY-FOUR

Billie

February 22, 1945

Isabella held her arms out to Billie. "Hossie?"

Billie plopped down on the Garcias' porch. "Okay. One time." She lifted Isabella onto her leg to give the requested horsie ride that had become their tradition. "This is the way the lady rides," Billie sang, moving her leg up and down gently. "Dumpty-dumpty-dum."

Isabella screeched. "Dumpty!"

Billie bobbed her leg faster. "And this is the way the gentleman rides. Dumpty-dumpty-dum."

"She's not going to be happy with just once." Tito barely looked up from his latest issue of *Sky and Telescope.*

"And this is the wa-ayy the farr-mer rides. Dumpty-dumpty-dum!" Billie bounced her leg side to side as if Isabella were mounted atop an old work-horse, jostling along.

Isabella laughed. "'Gin," she demanded.

"I told you." Tito turned another page in his magazine.

"How can I say no to her?" Billie asked, laughing.

Tito frowned at Isabella, pretending to be mad. "Billie's *my* friend," he said.

"Hossie!" Isabella wrapped her chubby arms around Billie's leg and held tight. She was one of the best parts of coming to Tito's house. Besides Tito. And Abuelita's homemade tortillas. And Mrs. Garcia calling her Saint Billie because of her ability to charm Isabella out of any tantrum.

Billie gave Isabella another "horsie" ride, then turned her loose. "Now Tito and I have to do school-work," she said.

"Mamá!" Isabella wailed.

Mrs. Garcia came to the door, clucking. "Bella, you must share Billie." She scooped the little girl up and took her inside, murmuring to her in Spanish.

"I used to be Bella's favorite," Tito said.

"Take a number." Billie felt on top of the world. Leo's latest letter said he was safe from the battles. Doff had allowed Bear into the kitchen to eat his supper. Billie's bedroom was not that far away. And now she had a best friend. "Ready to tackle our assignment?"

Tito picked up a small rucksack. "What does it look like?"

"Okay, then." Billie whistled for Bear. "Let's go. I have to sit for Mrs. Stewart in an hour."

Bear ran ahead of them as they hiked beyond the avocado orchards. "Hey, look at this!" Billie bent over a feather. "Think it's from an owl?"

Tito pretended to hold up a magnifying glass. "Definitely owl. Ten extra-credit points. Pick it up."

"What if it has germs?"

Tito sighed. "Here." He fished a handkerchief from his pocket and handed it to her.

She used it to pick up the feather. "Miss Daley is going to love our report."

"You children must become acquainted with your local flora and fauna," Tito mimicked their teacher.

"I'd like to see Hazel and Kit find an owl feather." Billie carefully placed her discovery in a manila folder. Then she stuffed the hanky in her dungarees pocket.

"This isn't a competition."

"I know. I know." Still. Hazel hated being out of doors. Kit only cared about hairdos. And Spinner and Del were too dumb to create anything interesting. "I bet when we're famous, Miss Daley's going to get interviewed and she's going to say she always knew we would be successful."

Tito sneezed. "Stop dreaming and get to work." He consulted the list in his notebook. "We need five examples of flora and five of fauna."

Billie held the manila envelope above her head. "Here's our first flora!" she exclaimed.

"Fauna," Tito corrected. "Flora has to do with plants."

"I knew that." Billie tucked the envelope in her book bag. Bear sat down to scratch behind his ear. "Look!" She wiggled a burr out of the ruff of Bear's neck. "Flora!"

Tito sighed. "Yes. Flora. But what type?"

"Isn't identification your job?"

"This is a team project," Tito reminded her.

"Okay. Okay." She tucked the burr into the envelope with the feather. "I'll look it up when we get home."

They hiked along, collecting samples while Bear snuffled, explored, and left his mark.

"We'd better head back soon," Billie said, stretching to get the kinks out of her back. "I can't be late for my babysitting job."

"We only have two more samples to collect," Tito said. "I think I saw a cactus over that way." He started off. Bear followed.

"We can finish this weekend!" Billie hollered after him. "I need to get going."

But Tito didn't answer.

Billie stamped her foot. "Bear. Get back here! You're my dog!"

Neither boy nor dog replied.

Billie trudged after them. "Mrs. Stewart's expecting me!" she hollered.

She stopped to listen for them. In the near distance, she heard jumbled voices. "Come on, you two.

Let's head back," she called, as the sounds led her up a small rise and down the other side.

There were Spinner and Del, on horseback.

"You're trespassing!" Spinner hollered at Tito. "This is our land."

Billie scrambled to catch up. "We're just out walking," she said.

Spinner's horse pranced left, then right. "Oh, I see. You two are walking. Together." He looked over at Del. "Bet Doff won't be none too happy about Billie's greaser boyfriend."

Billie ran at Spinner so fast that his horse lurched back a few steps. "He's not my boyfriend and you know it. We're working on the science project."

"Science project." Del sounded like a snake oil salesman.

"How do you say that in Spanish?" Spinner spit in Tito's direction.

Tito didn't react. Didn't say anything.

Spinner nudged his horse closer to Tito. Billie ran between them, waving her arms. Bear lunged between her and the horse, growling.

"Call that dog off," Spinner said. "Or I'll have the sheriff take him away."

"The sheriff should take you away." Billie glanced at a nearby fence post. "You say we're trespassing." She pointed at the post. "That's my aunt's mark. Rancho Vecinos. This is our land."

She looked over at Tito. What was wrong with him? Why wasn't he speaking up?

"I didn't see that before." Spinner tugged on the reins. "It's easy to get mixed up out here. Sometimes you think you're on your own land. And sometimes you think you can be friends with greasers." His horse pranced backward. "Come on, Del. Let's get out of here. It stinks of beans."

"Beans." Del turned to follow.

They were scarcely out of sight before Billie hollered. "What is wrong with you?" She picked up a stick at her feet and chucked it as far as she could. Bear barreled after it. "Why do you let them insult you that way?"

Bear bounded back, stick in mouth. He dropped it at Billie's feet. Furious, she tossed it again.

"Aren't you going to say anything?" she asked Tito.

"Do you ever listen to Mrs. Roosevelt?" He crouched down, watching Bear run. "She says that no one can make you feel inferior without your consent."

"That's just fine." Billie shook her head. "You are so full of what other people say. Thomas Edison. Henry Ford. Eleanor Roosevelt. What in the blazes do *you* say?"

Bear loped back, stick in mouth. He wagged his head from Billie to Tito.

"Here, Bear," Billie said.

He hesitated.

She glared at Tito. "Just because I try to stand up for myself doesn't make me inferior."

"I didn't mean that—"

"Yes. Yes, you did." Billie jumped up, grabbing Bear's stick. "Well, maybe I don't want to be a namby-pamby. Like you."

Tito flinched as if Billie's words had been boulders, catching him square in the chest. "If this is how you treat your friends, no wonder you don't have any."

She thought she might break into a million pieces right there if she didn't move. "Come, Bear." She ran. They ran.

Leaving Tito behind.

PART THREE

"I would rather walk with a friend in the dark,
than alone in the light."

—Helen Keller

CHAPTER TWENTY-FIVE

Billie

Still February 22, 1945

"Bear! Bear!" Stanley ran outside. "Momma saved a bone for you."

"And hello to you, too," Billie said.

"Oh, hi, Billie." Stanley threw his arms around Bear's neck. "Didi's crying."

Billie left Bear and Stanley playing chase in the yard and went inside. "Private Packer reporting for duty!" She covered her ears to drown out Didi's wails.

Mrs. Stewart, with Didi nested on her hip, came out to meet her. "Tragedy." She tried to set Didi down. "MuMu Monkey lost an ear."

Didi howled louder.

Billie kicked off her Keds. "Well, I bet some

cookies would make things better. What do you say, Didi? Shall we bake some cookies?"

"Ear!" Didi howled.

Mrs. Stewart raised an eyebrow. "Maybe I should stay home from my meeting," she said.

Leo had been sending Billie money each month for war stamps; she was counting on today's babysitting money to finish up her first booklet. Then she could trade it in for a twenty-five-dollar savings bond. "I bet we can figure something out." She tickled Didi's feet. "Is there a sewing kit around here?"

Mrs. Stewart nodded.

Billie brushed her hands together. "Right, then. Dr. Packer is ready to operate."

Didi stopped howling.

"Nurse." Billie held out her hand to Mrs. Stewart. "My surgical tools, please."

Didi sniffled. "Fix MuMu?" She let her mother set her down.

Mrs. Stewart brought Billie a sewing basket. "Oh, doctor. Only you can save the patient!" She opened the kit and set it on the table.

"Is there someone to assist?" Billie asked.

"Sist?" Didi rubbed her damp cheeks.

"Help. Can you help me?" Billie opened the sewing kit and pulled out needle and thread. "Very important."

Didi hurried to Billie's side. "I can sist."

Mrs. Stewart eased toward the front door.

Billie pulled out a length of thread. "Snip here." She held the scissors so Didi could make the cut. "Nicely done, nurse."

Mrs. Stewart pulled her hat off the hook and pinned it on top of her curls.

"Now, where is the patient?" Billie looked around.

"I get!" Didi ran for her bedroom, returning with the one-eared stuffed monkey.

"Nurse, please hold the patient very still," Billie said.

Mrs. Stewart turned the front doorknob. Paused.

"Ready for the first stitch?" Billie asked.

"MuMu is brave," Didi said. "Bye, Momma."

"Bye, dear." The door snicked shut behind Mrs. Stewart.

"I think the patient is going to pull through just fine." Billie ran the needle and thread over and over through the stuffed toy's head, reconnecting the ear. "Nearly finished." She knotted the thread and snipped it off. "There you go. Good as new."

Didi clasped MuMu to her. "I wanna show Stanley."

Billie held up her hand. "The patient must stay inside today. He may have a few bananas and some tea. But otherwise, he must nap."

"I can make tea!" Didi jumped up. "And bananas." She tended her recovering monkey, making endless cups of tea with her play tea set and serving pretend mashed bananas with a tablespoon.

MuMu seemed quite pleased at the attention.

After half an hour or so, Billie glanced outside. There was Bear, sleeping in the shade. But no sign of Stanley.

"Dr. Packer prescribes fresh air for the patient!" Billie scooped up Didi and MuMu and ran outside. "Stanley!" she called. "Where are you?"

His trike was parked in the front yard. She hollered his name again.

"Shhh!" Didi squished MuMu to her chest. "You're hurting his sore ear."

How far could Stanley have gotten away in the time she'd been playing doctor with Didi?

His jacket hung from the handlebars of the trike. Billie had never tried anything like this before, but she was desperate. She held the jacket to Bear's nose. He sniffed. "Go." She repeated. "Find."

Bear loped off. Billie couldn't leave Didi behind. She set girl and monkey in Mrs. Stewart's Victory Garden wheelbarrow.

"Fresh-air therapy!" Billie declared as they bumped along. "Hang on!"

Whenever Bear got out of sight, Billie whistled and he came back. But never with Stanley. Her heart pounded harder with each passing minute. "Stanley!" she called.

"Stanley!" Didi parroted.

After what seemed like days, Bear barked three times. He ran back to her, as if saying, *Come this way*. She swung Didi out of the wheelbarrow. "Piggyback ride!" she announced. Then she raced as fast as she could with a toddler clinging to her back. Bear led her to the bottom of a ditch. And Stanley.

Relief turned Billie's legs into Jell-O. "You're not supposed to leave the yard."

"I found an arrowhead!" Stanley held out his prize as he climbed toward her.

Billie inhaled. Tried to calm herself. No need to let Stanley know how terrified she'd been. "That is quite the find," she said. "Let's take it home to show your mother." *And let's not tell her how long you were gone,* she thought to herself.

The trek to the house took forever as Billie pushed the wheelbarrow, now laden with two children and one stuffed monkey. A blister sprouted up on her right heel. And her arms quivered with exhaustion as she fought to keep the wheelbarrow upright on the rutted terrain.

"I don't like this bumpy ride," Didi whined. "I want Momma!"

Billie felt like crying, too. She paused to catch her breath. "But, my lady," she panted, "the chariot is going as fast as it can."

Didi sniffled. "Chariot?"

"A golden one." Billie began pushing again. "As befits a princess."

"I *am* a princess." Didi held up MuMu. "And this is my pet dragon."

"I'm a knight." Stanley played along. "Sir Arrowhead."

"I'm Princess Petals." Didi waved an imaginary wand in Billie's direction. "And you are my horse, Roscoe."

"And he is my gallant steed, Smokey," Stanley added, pointing to Bear.

Billie neighed and Didi laughed. They kept up the game all the way home. Billie helped the kids out of the wheelbarrow and into the house.

"I'm hungry," Didi said.

"I'm thirsty." Stanley set his arrowhead on the table and sat admiring it.

Mrs. Stewart's icebox held some icy cold Nehi sodas. She'd said Billie could help herself. But the kids weren't allowed to drink them. Rather than fight that battle, Billie poured everyone a glass of water, filling a bowl for Bear.

"Someone's knocking!" Didi announced.

Billie glanced at the clock. Mrs. Stewart wasn't due home for another half an hour or so. And she wouldn't knock, anyway.

She peered through the front curtains.

A telegram deliveryman stood on the front porch. "Telegram for Mrs. Robert Stewart," he announced.

"She's, uh, indisposed," Billie called out.

The man's feet shuffled on the porch. "I've got lots of deliveries today. Let me slide this under the door."

The telegram shussed over the threshold and onto the linoleum. Billie didn't pick it up right away. Her legs got wobbly again, as if she were still push-ing the wheelbarrow. All she could think about was the telegram she'd found in the dictionary. Cautiously, Billie set this one on the kitchen table, next to Stanley's arrowhead.

It could be good news. Telegrams were sent all the time to congratulate people on anniversaries or to let them know company was coming. Maybe it was Mrs. Stewart's birthday. Maybe she'd won a con-test. Maybe her sister had a baby. Billie couldn't think of any more maybes.

"Can I have some crackers?" Stanley asked.

Billie took a tin from the cupboard.

"Those aren't crackers," Stanley said. "That's tea."

Before she could switch out the tins, the front door opened. "I'm home!"

Billie froze.

"Momma! Look what I found!" Stanley grabbed the arrowhead, knocking the telegram to the floor.

Mrs. Stewart entered the kitchen. "How did everything go?" she asked, smoothing hair mussed by unpinning her hat. Her face drained when she saw the small tan envelope. "Billie, would you take the children outside for a moment?"

Billie organized a game of hide-and-seek. "No fair," Stanley said. "Bear keeps finding me."

"How about tag, then?" Billie halfheartedly chased them around the yard, one eye on the door, waiting for Mrs. Stewart to come out.

When she did, her face was composed. Calm. But white as chalk. "Say good-bye to Billie, children."

"We were having fun!" Stanley complained.

"Yeah. Fun." Didi stomped her little foot.

"I'll be back soon," Billie promised. "Go on. Mind your mom." She didn't know what to say. "Is everything all right?" she finally asked.

Mrs. Stewart's lips trembled. A huge tear dribbled down her cheek. "I'm afraid we got some dreadful news." She hugged the children to her. "We'll see you later, dear." The door closed.

Billie hoped she never saw that look on anyone's face ever again. She didn't know what to do.

But she knew who would.

Doff.

Billie sprinted away, Bear at her side. She kept blinking the tears away so she could see where she was running. As she got close to the ranch house, she screamed, "Doff! Doff!"

The front door swung open and Doff stepped out, drying her hands on her apron. "What on earth?"

Billie collapsed in her great-aunt's arms, spilling the news along with more tears.

Doff half carried her inside. Within minutes, there was a cup of hot, sweetened tea in front of Billie. And Doff was on the telephone, one comforting hand on Billie's shoulder, organizing the neighborhood.

Billie stared into her teacup, unable to take one sip.

Now Stanley would never get the present his dad had promised to send.

CHAPTER TWENTY-SIX

Billie

Doff arranged for Stanley and Didi to stay with Hazel's family for a few nights, because her younger brothers were close to Stanley's age. Then she called to offer Mrs. Stewart the spare room at Rancho Vecinos. "I see. I see," Doff said into the receiver.

"No, dear. I honestly do understand. Sometimes it is good to be alone." She replaced the receiver, looking off into space. Billie wondered if she was thinking back to when she'd gotten a similar telegram. She tried to think of something to say to her aunt, but nothing came. After a few moments, Doff snapped out of it, grabbing her apron. "Well, that meat loaf won't make itself."

The phone had been ringing off the hook with neighbors volunteering food and help. It rang again, but Doff was up to her elbows, mixing ground beef and onions. "Grab that, will you? And if it's Sylvia Lesser, ask her to make that molded salad of hers. It sits easy on a sad stomach."

It wasn't Mrs. Lesser, but Mrs. Garcia. "Would you care to speak to my aunt?" Billie said.

"No, thank you." Mrs. Garcia's voice sounded flat over the phone. "Tito is not home."

"He's not?" Billie turned the cord around her finger. "Maybe he decided to stay out collecting samples. I had to leave to babysit." Mrs. Garcia didn't need to know all the details.

"His father is out looking for him." Mrs. Garcia's voice cracked. "If you hear anything, please let us know."

"I will." Billie replaced the receiver. She thought she might throw up. Tito should have been home hours ago. This was her fault. Her fault.

"Who was that?" Doff pressed the meat mixture into a pair of loaf pans.

"Oh. Um." Billie didn't dare look at her great-aunt. "Hazel wondered if I'd come help with Didi." Billie slipped on her Keds. "That okay with you?"

"Of course." Doff slid the loaf pans into the oven. "If I'm not here when you get back, it's because I'm delivering dinner to Mrs. Stewart."

Billie whistled and Bear came running. She wanted to fall to her knees and cry into that black fur, but there wasn't a second to waste on a pity party. She tore off toward the avocado orchard. Tito had a terrible sense of direction. He could be anywhere. She stopped. How was she going to find him? By now, he could be clear to Camp Pendleton. This was hopeless.

She jammed her hands in her pockets. In the left one was a handkerchief. Tito's handkerchief. She thought about Bear tracking Stanley.

She held out the hanky, praying it had enough of Tito's scent. "Bear. Find."

Bear poked his nose at the fabric, sniffing.

"Got it?" she asked.

Bear shook himself.

She issued the next command with her whole heart. "Find Tito."

Bear led the way, as they pounded past the barn and corral, past the orchards and beyond. Every now and again, Bear would sniff the ground and change direction. But they were mostly moving toward the setting sun, heading west.

"We were over there," she said, pointing in the opposite direction. "I think he'd be that way." She paused, panting.

But Bear ignored her outstretched hand and kept moving.

"Stupid astronomer!" Billie shivered in the cooling air. "No sense of direction!" Why hadn't she brought a coat? She stumbled on some loose rock going down a small hill and turned her ankle. She hobbled a few steps. It hurt like the dickens. But there wasn't anything to do but run. So she did.

Sometimes, Bear would get so far ahead, she wasn't sure which way to go. A whistle would bring him bounding back to her. They ran on, and on, and on. Bending to ease a stitch in her side, she wondered how much farther she could go.

Why had she been so mean? Tito was no namby-pamby. He was the bravest person she knew. And the smartest. Who cared what Spinner said or thought? That lout wasn't worth her breath. Tito had been right about that all along.

He'd even made that leash for her because he knew she didn't have the money to buy one. She'd never had a friend like that before. She might never again. "Tito!" she screamed.

Bear paused to sniff a shrub.

"Denny said you were supposed to help me." She sobbed out the words. "Please. Help me find Tito."

Bear barked once, then surged ahead again. When she lost sight of him, she whistled. He didn't come back. She whistled again. "Bear! Here!"

She bent over, pressing against the stitch in her side. She didn't know how she could keep going.

Then she heard a barking in the distance. She jabbed her fingers into her stomach; the stitch was now a knife blade of pain and nothing relieved it. But she couldn't stop.

At the top of a ravine, Bear paced and barked.

She scrambled to reach him. What was he barking at? The vegetation was so dense, an elephant could be hiding down there. "What is it, boy?"

Her eye caught light glinting off glass.

"Tito!" she called.

Billie scouted around to find a passable trail down the ravine. Maybe there? She slipped and slid, bare arms shredded by sharp twigs and prickers. She yelped in pain when she cracked her shin on a rock, but didn't even stop to wipe at the blood. She fought her way down, calling Tito's name over and over.

When she was about to give up, Bear bolted ahead to a low spot between two pines. He stopped, sniffing at something. A very still something.

Tito.

CHAPTER TWENTY-SEVEN

Denny

February 19 to February 22, 1945

"There's air power up there to handle that machine gun," Sergeant Manuelito said. "Let these guys ask for help."

The CO frowned. "There's no time."

Denny and Jesse were already getting out the radio and the headsets. "Give us a chance," Denny said.

The CO scratched his stubble. Seconds ticked by. They all knew they couldn't keep doing what they were doing. Not if anyone was going to survive. "What the heck's our location?" the CO asked. Someone gave him the coordinates and he rattled off a message. "Send it," he ordered.

Jesse cranked. Denny transmitted. "Arizona! Arizona!" he shouted into the mouthpiece, trying to be heard over the din. He gave their location coordinates and the request for air support. *"Gah, ne-ahs-jah."* Roger and Out.

Then he held his breath, eyes trained on the skies above.

"Look!" Manuelito shouted.

A half dozen Allied planes spun into view. Before the men could even cheer, the machine gun was out of commission. Manuelito patted Denny and Jesse on the back. "That bought us some breathing room," he said.

"Stick with me." The CO started off. "This way."

In tandem, Denny and Jesse moved their equipment where ordered. All through that horrific day and the next, they took turns cranking the radio, encoding and decoding messages. Sweat stung their eyes. Smoke burned their nostrils. Still they cranked. Received. Translated. Cranked. Translated. Sent. Over and over again. It was worse than the worst nightmare Denny had ever dreamed in his life.

At nightfall the second night, they sought shelter in shell holes, trying to get a little sleep. Fleas feasted on bare skin. Rats scuttled over and around them as they did their best to get comfortable in the ashy damp. They kept their boots on so at least they didn't have to worry about some critter taking up housekeeping there in the cool of the night.

Denny dozed off, then startled awake, nauseated that his nightmare was reality. There would be no forgetting the terrors of this place. Iwo Jima was a scar he would bear for the rest of his life. However long that might be.

Then it began again. The sweat, the smoke, the cries for help.

The enemy was wily. Dug in. Determined. Hour by hour, the medics carried litters of wounded back to the boats. Hour by hour, fresh graves were dug.

Denny stopped counting the moments when he didn't think he could take one more step. Crank the radio one more time. Encode one more message. Decode one more message. Because there was no choice but to keep stepping, keep cranking, keep sending and receiving messages.

Otherwise, all would be lost.

CHAPTER TWENTY-EIGHT

|||||||||||||||||||||||||||||||||||||||||||||||||||||||||||||||||||||||||||||||||||||||||||||||||||||||||

Billie

Was he breathing? And should an arm even be in that position?

Bear positioned himself at Tito's head.

"Tito?" She called his name softly this time.

"Papá?" Tito mumbled. His left hand reached out.

She touched it gently. "Where are you hurt?"

"My arm." Tito's eyes fluttered. "Did I break my glasses?"

"No. They look okay." He felt so cold. Why hadn't she grabbed a coat? Then she could cover him, keep him warm. "We need to get you out of here."

When he tried to sit up, his face blanched whiter. "I'm gonna be sick," he moaned.

"Okay. Okay. Just lie there for a minute." Billie sat back on her haunches. In the movies, she would cut some pine branches and lash them together to make a stretcher. But this was real life. There was no way she could carry him up that steep embankment.

Bear jumped to a standing position, ears on alert.

"Do you hear someone?" Maybe they'd been found. Billie jumped up. "Help!" She waved her arms. "Help! We're down here."

Bear howled, as if helping to broadcast her SOS.

There was no response.

Bear howled again. It sounded like his big dog heart was breaking. He paced around and around and around. His agitation made Billie even more nervous. "Quiet. Down," she commanded.

But he kept pacing.

A huge clap of thunder sounded in the distance. No wonder he was nervous.

Oh, it couldn't rain. Not on top of everything else. No rain. "It's okay, boy." She reached out to pat him, more to calm herself than him. Bear turned, and licked her hand.

Another crack of thunder. So loud that Billie covered her ears.

And in that moment, Bear took off.

She lunged afer him. "Here. Here." But he kept running. Away from them. Toward the west. "Bear!"

In a blink, her dog was completely out of sight.

And she was alone, all alone, with Tito.

His chest still moved up and down. But that arm. And his face. Now it was the color of the ashes she emptied from the ranch house fireplace. Tito moaned again.

"I'm here." She reached out to pat him but jerked her hand back. What if she made him worse?

He muttered a short string of words in Spanish.

"What?" She leaned over him. "I couldn't hear you."

He didn't answer, even after she repeated her question.

Billie wiped her damp eyes. They were at the bottom of a ravine. No one knew they were there. And night was falling.

"Help!" Billie tipped her head back and screamed from the depths of her soul. "Help us!"

Bear was gone, in the wrong direction. And there was no one else.

No one but Billie.

CHAPTER TWENTY-NINE

Billie

Billie broke off some pine branches and placed them gently over Tito. She wished she could make a more comfortable bed for him to rest on, but she was terrified to move him. He hadn't said anything for quite a while, but he was still breathing. She checked that every few minutes.

With the darkening sky came cooler air. Billie shivered as she added another layer of limbs to Tito's makeshift blanket. Could he survive a night outside?

He mumbled something again. *"Gracias,"* he said. "Thank you."

She knelt by him. "I'm so sorry. I was a jerk." She was more than a jerk. It was her fault he was here. That he was hurt. Why couldn't she keep her big trap shut?

"You were." He closed his eyes. "But what's a little jerkiness between friends?"

Billie sniffled. "Are we? Friends?"

"I think so." His forehead wrinkled from pain. "Thanks for finding me."

"Well, that was Bear." Billie stopped. She remembered Denny's words that first night. Bear truly had helped her find what she was looking for. A real friend. Tito.

He shifted under the boughs and then cried out. "I guess I can't move that way." He coughed. "I really don't feel good."

She drew in a deep breath. Made a decision. "I think the highway's about half a mile away. I'm going for help."

He shook his head, moaning. "What if no one comes by?"

"They will." She layered more pine boughs over him. "They have to."

It was a pickup truck that stopped for her, with Mr. Greeley behind the wheel. He didn't bat an eye but drove like a madman to the Garcias'. "Hop in!" he hollered to Mr. Garcia. Billie grabbed blankets and towels while Mr. Garcia loaded four-by-fours and rope into the bed of Mr. Greeley's truck.

"Stay here," Mrs. Garcia said to Billie. "You are freezing."

But she wasn't about to leave her friend out there. Besides, she had to point out the way. So Tito's big sister loaned her a jacket and she hopped back in the truck cab. Though it seemed to take hours, the clock on the dashboard showed fifteen minutes passed before they reached the ravine. The men rigged up a stretcher with the lumber and rope.

"Tito!" Billie scrambled down the ravine. "I brought your dad!"

"Papá" was the only word Tito said as Mr. Greeley and Mr. Garcia loaded him onto the makeshift stretcher.

"Here." Billie took the dish towel she'd borrowed from Mrs. Garcia to make a sling so Tito's bad arm wouldn't bounce any more than could be helped. They tied him on to the stretcher so he wouldn't fall off on the steep incline. Inch by inch, the two men hauled the heavy makeshift stretcher and its cargo back to the truck. When Mr. Garcia got Tito settled in the bed, he slapped the cab to signal "go." Mr. Greeley floored it to the hospital.

There was a flurry of nurses and doctors. Mr. Greeley bought Billie some hot chocolate from a vending machine in the hall. Then he disappeared. When he came back, he tapped Billie's knee with his cap. "His father's going to stay with him tonight," he said. "I'll take you home."

"Can I see him first?" Billie said.

Mr. Greeley shook his head. "They gave him something so he'd sleep. Best let him be. I'll bring you over here tomorrow if no one else can." They walked to the truck.

Billie was too exhausted to even think about the fact that she'd been riding with Spinner's father. Now she paused with her hand on the door handle. She should probably say something. But what?

They both climbed into the cab.

"You have quite the left hook, I hear." Mr. Greeley turned the key in the ignition.

"What?" Billie shook her head. "Oh, I didn't mean to hurt Spinner. I just—" She sighed. "I did want to hurt him, I think. To make him stop being mean."

Mr. Greeley gave the old truck a little gas. "I know. Doff called and explained everything."

"She did?" Billie nearly slid off the bench seat.

"You know bloody noses don't solve much," he said.

"I really do." She scrubbed at her eyes. "I am so sorry."

They rode along in silence. Mr. Greeley turned off the highway onto the long drive to Rancho Vecinos. He idled in front of the house. "You were one brave girl tonight," he said.

Billie did not feel the least bit brave. She closed the truck door. "Thank you. Good night."

She headed up the front porch steps. Doff was going to blow her top. And she probably deserved it.

Billie paused and glanced over her shoulder.

She whistled, even though she didn't expect a response.

CHAPTER THIRTY

Denny

February 23, 1945

Denny leaned his back against Jesse's in the fox-hole. "Catch some shut-eye," he said.

Jesse was snoring in an instant.

Since the landing three days before, sleep had come in twenty-minute stretches at best. Denny had learned to doze through the gunfire and shelling; what kept him awake now were the silences.

What was happening out there? He'd seen men tip their heads inches above improvised foxholes only to find those same men later, unmoving, caught by a sniper's bullet. Had they stood to stretch? To pray? The reason would never be known. The reality was another grave.

His stomach grumbled. Growled. Moving slowly to avoid disturbing Jesse, Denny unwrapped a chunk of Hershey bar and gnawed at it. It didn't resemble any of the candy he'd bought at the trading post as a kid, but it was food.

He let the waxy bite melt as slowly as possible, willing the trickles to fill the empty crevasses in his belly. Jesse jerked in his sleep, snorted, then settled again. Denny closed his eyes; maybe the chocolate would help quiet his stomach, let him get some rest.

Moments later, Denny jerked awake at a sound in the foxhole. He shifted around with his Ka-Bar knife in hand. Looking. Listening. Please don't let it be another rat. He really hated rats. He stared into the dark, tightening his grip on the knife handle.

Whatever it was didn't make a sound as it crept closer. Denny tensed, poised to thrust knife into flesh.

A jagged line of white flashed against a black shadow.

Was that the thump of a heavy tail?

He rubbed his eyes, then blinked hard. It couldn't be.

Bear?

Denny certainly wasn't the only one who'd been seeing things; before Jesse fell asleep, he'd insisted that the hunk of rock he held was an icy cold bottle of Coca-Cola.

Even if was a hallucination, Denny couldn't help whispering again, "Bear?"

He reached out his hand and it passed through the shadow. There was no substance. No black furry body. No swishing tail.

The sense of loss slammed Denny's hopes to the earth. The pain was excruciating. Worse than when the matron chopped off his hair. Worse than being forced to suck on Fels-Naphtha for speaking his own language. Worse than being locked in the basement for running away from the boarding school.

He had so wanted there to be a warm furry something in the dark. After the horrors of the past few days, was it too much to ask? He curled up like a baby. There was no way he could go on. "I'm sorry," he whispered to Jesse. Denny folded in on himself, feeling as if he could fit his entire being into the buckskin pouch that hung around his neck. A pouch he'd hardly opened since giving Billie that bit of turquoise. He felt happy about having done that. At least a bit of him would live on.

Denny stretched. All he had to do was stand. Stand up. And it would be over. Slowly, he began to uncurl his limbs.

As he did, his arm was brushed with a cool dampness. A dog nose kiss. He pressed his fingers to the spot, as if receiving a blessing. Then something licked his face. He had no idea how it could be possible, but he felt the damp swipe of a tongue.

He sat back down in the foxhole. Curled up again, out of range of fire. For the first time in weeks, Denny relaxed. He dozed peacefully until dawn, when he caught a glimpse of a black furry head leaning into the foxhole, pink tongue lolling to the side.

It was Bear. It could only be Bear.

Why he was there, Denny had no idea. But in the dog's eyes, he saw his *cheii*, his grandfather. There was a smile. A welcoming wave home. Denny waved back. "Thank you, Grandfather," he said. "Thank you, Bear."

As the sun chased the dark from the sky, Jesse shifted awake, too. He loosened the pouch at his neck to take out a pinch of corn pollen.

Denny did the same. He reached for the medicine bag at his neck and brought out a small pinch of corn pollen.

"In beauty it is begun." Jesse spoke the words quietly.

Denny recited the prayer with his friend, the last words a whisper: "In beauty it is ended." These familiar words came so easily. Denny had tried to ignore this part of his life. But these past few days had shown him he could be both Marine and Diné. No: *must* be both. He touched a bit of pollen to his tongue, asking for help in sending and receiving messages quickly and accurately.

"We're going to make it," Jesse said as they strapped on their rifles.

Denny nodded. Then he silently said one last prayer, in gratitude for the vision that he knew his grandfather had sent to him, the vision that had made itself known. The vision of Bear.

"Smith. Begay!" The CO called their names. "Head toward Mount Suribachi," he ordered. "They need a radio up there."

Denny gave Jesse a thumbs-up as he grabbed his gear.

"I'm right behind you," Jesse said.

And so they headed for the mountain. Jesse following Denny.

And Denny following Bear.

CHAPTER THIRTY-ONE

Billie

"I can see why you love this place." Tito touched the top of Elephant Rock. "You can see forever."

Billie turned off the flashlight she'd carried. "Wait a minute and I'll spread out the blanket." She shook it out and placed it just so. "Okay, have a seat."

"Look at those stars!" Tito fumbled to get his binoculars out of his bag. "I'm still not used to this darned cast." He finally got the strap around his neck. He held out the binoculars. "Maybe you should look first?"

"No. You're the astronomer."

She settled herself on the blanket, too, while Tito fiddled with knobs to focus. Even in the dark she couldn't help herself. She leaned forward, not looking skyward along with Tito, but out, across to the highway. This time she wasn't looking for a father but a four-legged friend.

"Are you hungry?" Tito asked, eyes still glued to the eyepieces. "Abuelita sent tortillas," he said. "In the rucksack there."

Billie found a foil packet, unwrapping it to reveal a flour tortilla, spread with butter and cinnamon and rolled into a doughy scroll. Without thinking, she broke off a bite, holding it out for Bear.

"I guess I'll wait." She wrapped the tortilla back up. Then she pulled her knees to her chest, staring hard at the night sky to keep the tears from forming. One star seemed to wink at her. "Star light, star bright, grant the wish I wish tonight." She closed her eyes.

"You've got to take a look at this." Tito handed over the binoculars. "Adjust the focus here."

She pressed the eyepieces to her face. Moved the focus dial. "Oh!" She tilted her head back. "That's beautiful."

"Orion the hunter," Tito said. "Can you pick out his belt? Three stars in a row?"

Billie stared so hard she felt dizzy. "Yes. I think I can. What are those stars beside him? To his left?"

"His dogs." Tito slapped his leg. "Oh, I'm sorry. I didn't mean to—"

Billie pulled the binoculars away. "Here, you should have a turn."

She couldn't see his face but she knew Tito felt bad. It wasn't his fault Bear left. And it wasn't his fault that there was a jagged, dog-sized hole in her heart that would never heal up. Billie had been so blue that Doff even offered to get her another dog. But there was no other dog.

"So." Billie scratched her neck, thinking about a way to change the subject. "How do you know about all this?" She waved her arm at the sky.

"Lots of times, when we worked in the fields, we'd have to sleep outside. Field mice ran over our feet in the dark. Owls swooped over our heads. Once, I even got dive-bombed by a bat!"

Billie shivered. "That would give me the heebie-jeebies."

"I had a hard time sleeping. Then one night, Abuelita pointed out the Big Bear constellation. She said he was watching over me. That he wouldn't let anything happen." Tito shifted on the blanket. "After that, the night didn't seem so scary. Because, you know. The stars were up there watching over me." He put the binoculars back up to his face. "Galileo said, 'I have loved the stars too fondly to be fearful of the night.' After Abuelita told me about the constellations, I stopped being afraid at night."

"It is beautiful." Billie lay back on the blanket, looking up.

"Of course, I still get the willies every time I see a bat," Tito confessed.

"Don't start." She bolted upright. "You'll have me hearing bats, too." She pulled her feet onto the blanket. "What are some other constellation names?"

"Well, it depends," Tito answered.

"What?" she teased. "You're not the expert after all?"

"All I meant was, it depends on who's asking. For example"—he pointed upward—"we call that constellation Casseiopia's Chair."

"I know."

"But Denny calls it Northern Female. Well, I mean, the Navajo call it that. And—" Tito pointed to the North Star. "That's North Fire. And I bet other cultures have other names, too."

Billie leaned back on her elbows. It was like Leo said: It was a big world out there.

"Are you going to eat your tortilla?" Tito pulled it out of the rucksack. "I'm hungry enough to eat mine and yours."

She smiled. It was good that he was hungry. Meant he was healing. "Take it."

The scent of cinnamon hit her nose, and her mouth watered a little. Didn't matter. There would be other star-watching nights. Other chances to eat Abuelita's tortillas.

"You are one noisy chewer," she commented.

"I'm not chewing now," Tito said.

"Then what's that I hear?"

"It's too loud for a bat." She felt him tense. "Sounds like something bigger."

"Like what?" She jerked up the edges of the blanket. "Should we get out of here?"

"If it's a coyote—"

"A coyote!" Billie jumped up. Something thrashed through the underbrush.

"Abuelita says it's going to be more afraid of us than we are of it," Tito finished.

"Let's go." Billie picked up the rucksack.

"Where's the flashlight?" Tito asked.

Billie fumbled around in the dark. She found the flashlight and shone it in the direction of the crashing sounds. The beam picked up two glowing eyes. "Tito," her voice wavered.

He stood, too, but before they could move, the creature was on them.

Licking them like crazy.

CHAPTER THIRTY-TWO

Denny

"You gotta leave me." Jesse pressed his hand to the wound on his side. His shirtsleeve had been torn away. Denny could barely see the Marine emblem tattoo on his forearm for all the blood. "A medic will be along soon."

Following Bear's lead, they had dodged bullets and shells and booby traps as they climbed Mount Suribachi. Then, yards from where they were to set up, Bear vanished. Moments later, Jesse got hit.

Denny knew the drill as well as Jesse did. Nothing stopped a message from getting through. Nothing. Marines did their jobs. No questions asked.

"Go." Jesse coughed. "Go."

Denny thought of the times his mother had carried home the one lost lamb. The one wayward goat. She had trained Denny to be strong. She had trained him to protect the land. And his people. He was a Marine. And he was Diné.

"You're coming with me." With his radio and rifle banging against his back, and his friend in his arms, Denny ran.

When he thought he could go no farther, Denny reached the transmission point. He set Jesse down and got out the radio. Jesse cranked with his good arm. And Denny relayed the message they'd been given.

Because they were sitting ducks once a message had been sent—the enemy could home in on their signal—Denny picked Jesse up and they scrambled away. Farther up the mountain, they tumbled into a ditch with some other Marines. One of them had a red cross on his sleeve.

"Medic!" Denny called.

Soon, capable hands were administering to Jesse.

Radio in his lap, Denny leaned forward, weak with exhaustion.

"Will you look at that?" One of the Marines nudged him in the ribs.

Had he seen the vision, too? Denny glanced up, straining for a glimpse of black fur.

"Will you look at that?" the Marine repeated.

Denny looked. Five soldiers pushed a pole into the ground on the top of Mount Suribachi. The newly raised American flag snapped in the wind.

"We've done it," the Marine said.

Denny fell back against the ditch wall. Closed his eyes. Offered a prayer of thanks to the Creator.

For Bear.

CHAPTER THIRTY-THREE

Bear

The dog padded into the girl's bedroom where she sat at her desk, scratching a sharpened stick across a piece of paper. He curled up at her feet, worn out from chasing a rabbit out of the older woman's garden that afternoon.

The girl was tired, too. He sensed it even before she yawned.

"I'm beat." She snapped some kind of cover over the writing stick. "I can finish these letters tomorrow." He remained under the desk while she did the things humans do to prepare for sleep. She soon came back with minty breath and a face moist from washing. Bear took a moment himself to wash a spot on his front forepaw.

She pulled back blankets. He stood, stretched, and padded to the bedroom door, ready to move to his own comfortable sleeping place. He glanced back at the girl.

"Hey." She patted the spot next to her. "Come."

He paused. Blinked. This was new.

She patted again. "It's okay."

Bear shook himself. A dog's role was to obey.

It was not his place to disagree with his girl.

He leaped up, turning three times before settling near her feet.

The room grew dark.

"Good night, Bear," she said. "Don't let the bedbugs bite."

He didn't understand her words, but such details weren't necessary between friends. The sounds told him everything he needed to know.

The dog tucked his muzzle under his front paws and slept.

CHAPTER THIRTY-FOUR

Billie and Denny

The dust signaled the car's approach long before he heard it. That was the signal to put on a fresh pot of coffee. By the time the Chevy was in front of the hogan, the percolator was *bup-bup-bupping* on the stove. He stepped onto the porch and waved to the driver. She'd spent enough time on the reservation to know to wait for this invitation. The door opened and a woman in her forties hopped out. A big black dog followed close on her heels.

The dog, not one to stand on formality, ran to Denny, tail wagging. "Who's this?" he asked.

"Pilot." She held up a container. "I brought cookies."

"It's good to see you." He took her free hand as she reached the porch, shaking it. "Coffee's ready."

With cups in hand, they settled in his tidy living room.

"Leo's good," she offered.

Denny nodded. "Got a letter from him a while back."

They sipped, enjoying the coffee and the companionable silence.

After a time, she set her cup down and pulled a book out of her handbag. He could read the title from where he sat: *Navajo Code Talkers*. He'd not spoken with its author, but some of his friends had.

Billie patted the front cover. "This is your story, too, isn't it?"

Pilot had crossed the room to sniff out any stray cookie crumbs. Finding none, he snuffled, then rested his muzzle on Denny's knee.

"Push him away if he bothers you," Billie said.

Denny stroked the dog's black furry head. Remembered another black furry dog. "He's not bothering me one bit."

"I can't believe we never knew." Billie sat back, shaking her head. "That you never said anything."

"I don't know about being a code talker," he said. "We were radiomen."

She sighed. "Still."

"They told us not to tell." Denny scratched behind Pilot's ears. The dog closed his eyes and huffed, just as Bear had upon receiving that very same treatment.

"But the program was declassified five years ago." She threw up her hands. "Five years! You could have said something then."

"We were Marines. Doing a job."

She shook her head again, this time so vigorously that the silver-and-turquoise earrings at her ears jangled. "I can't get over it," she said. "When you were little, they tried to prevent you from speaking Navajo, and then the language ends up winning the war for us."

He shifted in his chair. "I wouldn't say that."

She grinned at him, and in that moment, he saw the eleven-year-old girl he'd met all those years ago. "Well, then, what *would* you say?" She crossed and uncrossed her legs. "I'm all ears."

The dog curled up at his feet, as if getting comfortable for a story, too.

Denny patted the pouch hanging from his neck,

thinking of the Blessingway prayer: "In beauty, all things end."

The Diné custom was to tell stories during the winter, when snow blanketed the ground. But Denny decided today he could make an exception.

For Billie.

Though I had tremendous input from people like Dr. Roy Hawthorne, one of the Navajo Code Talkers, and Michael Smith, son of Code Talker Samuel "Jesse" Smith, Sr., it is possible that I have made some mistakes in relating this story. I beg forgiveness in advance.

Would Billie and Denny likely have met and been friends? Who knows? In my worldview, they would have. It also seemed right to me that Bear would help the two people he most loved, no matter how many miles separated them. And, in case you're wondering, Bear is a Belgian shepherd.

I do not advocate alternate facts, but this *is* a work of fiction. The test in chapter 13, where Denny and Jesse compete against the cipher machine, reflects an actual test of the Navajo Code, which occurred much earlier in the war. In fact, even after the Navajo radiomen were in the field, their value continued to be questioned by some military higher-ups. Once their skills were recognized, the radiomen and their code ended up saving countless lives.

It is difficult to determine exactly how many Navajo Code Talkers there were; most sources identify an original 29. It seems likely that over 400 in all served in this capacity, perhaps closer to 420.

The Navajo spellings in this book are those used during WWII. When Denny was sending a message about a Torpedo Plane, for example, he would have transmitted: *tas-chizzie* (swallow). Today that word is spelled: *táshchozhii*. The modern spellings of the code words used in this book (and more) can be found in *Our Fathers, Our Grandfathers, Our Heroes . . . The Navajo Code Talkers of World War II*, a publication that accompanied a photographic exhibit by the same name, curated by Zonnie Gorman and Eunice Kahn.

It is hard to imagine in this age of social media, where no crumb of news goes unreported, that four hundred men could have done their job, and that was that. They were told not to tell anyone what they had done and they did not tell. Anyone. Not even their families. Perhaps, as some Code Talkers have said, they merely felt they were doing their duty. Perhaps, as others have said, they did not want to tell their stories lest the young think there was glamour in war. Either way, these responses are a testament to the greatness of these Marines who stepped up and served a country that had for so long ill-served them. And, in many ways, continues to do so.

It took the United States thirty-seven years to acknowledge the Code Talkers' contributions. The Navajo Code was declassified in 1968; finally, in 1982, President Ronald Regan declared August 14 Code Talkers Day. It wasn't until April 12, 2000—fifty-five years after the war had ended—that President Bill Clinton signed a law recognizing the original twenty-nine Code Talkers. In 2001, President George Bush presented Congressional Gold Medals to the surviving five originals—John Brown, Allen Dale June, Chester Nez, Lloyd Oliver, and Joe Palmer (represented by his son Kermit). Hundreds of others were honored with Congressional Silver Medals. In 2013, Congress honored the work of Code Talkers from other Tribes and nations, including the Apache, Cherokee, Chippewa, Choctaw, Comanche,

Creek, Crow, Fox, Hopi, Kiowa, Menominee, Mohawk, Oneida, Osage, Pawnee, Ponca, Pueblo, Sac, Seminole, Sioux, and Tlingit.

Soon, there will be no Code Talkers left alive. Let us never forget these brave, smart, selfless men. It is up to us to share the message of their story.

ACKNOWLEDGMENTS

||||||||||||||||||||||||||||||||||||||||||||||||||||||||||||||||||||||||

When I first began thinking about this book, Nancy Bo Flood was incredibly generous with information and resources. Dr. Roy Hawthorne, one of the four hundred Navajo Code Talkers, was helpful in setting my feet on the proper path. I wish he and I could have had more conversations, as he reminded me so much of my paternal grandfather.

Michael Smith, son of Samuel "Jesse" Smith, Sr., Code Talker, graciously agreed to read the Denny portions of this book. I am so grateful for his guidance, corrections, and encouragement. In honor of his kindness, and with his permission, I have named one of the characters in this book after his father, who fought on Iwo Jima and did indeed bear a tattoo on his forearm of the USMC emblem, with his Marine nickname, "Jesse," below.

Thanks to Dr. Stanley Burns, Wendy Dodson, Jennifer Holm, and Karen Lampe for help in identifying the ingredients of the anti-seasick pills that the Marines were given.

Thanks to Tricia Gardella, Kristi Hawthorne (no relation to Dr. Hawthorne), Mary Nethery, Quinn Wyatt, countless reference librarians, and the Marine Corps Association and Foundation for research assistance.

Books that guided my journey into this story: *Code Talker: The First and Only Memoir by One of the Original Navajo Code Talkers of WWII*, by Chester Nez, with Judith Schiess Avila; *Search for the Navajo Code Talkers*, by Sally McClain; *Warriors: Navajo Code Talkers*, photographs by Kenji Kawano; *Our Fathers, Our Grandfathers, Our Heroes . . . The Navajo Code Talkers of World War II*, text of the exhibit curated by the Circle of Light Navajo Educational Project, curators Zonnie Gorman and Eunice Kahn. Visit kirbylarson.com to see additional resources used in writing this book.

I have long wanted to shine a spotlight on the Navajo Code Talkers who served an ungrateful nation so valiantly and without hesitation. Thank you to my entire Scholastic family for affording me this opportunity: Jennifer Abbots, Julie Amitie, Lori Benton, Ellie Berger, Isa Caban, Michelle Campbell,

Rachel Feld, Emily Heddleson, David Levithan, Vaishali Nayak, Melissa Schirmer, Lizette Serrano, Brooke Shearouse, Mindy Stockfield, Tracy van Straaten, Olivia Valcarce, Dick Robinson; Alan Boyko, Jana Haussman, Robin Hoffman, and the whole Book Fair gang; and the Scholastic Reading Clubs. Thank you, Maeve Norton, for an irresistible cover.

Hugs to Jill Grinberg, agent extraordinaire, and her Brooklyn crew. Hugs to my family, who has to wonder what the heck Mom is doing when she could be babysitting the adorable Eli, Esme, Audrey, Clio, or Ryan. Hugs to Neil simply because. And if there is a Nobel Prize for best editor, ever, it must go to Lisa Sandell, who puts up with me. God only knows why.

ABOUT THE AUTHOR

Kirby Larson is the acclaimed author of the Newbery Honor book *Hattie Big Sky*; its sequel, *Hattie Ever After*; the historical romp *Audacity Jones to the Rescue* and its sequel, *Audacity Jones Steals the Show*; *The Friendship Doll*; Dear America: *The Fences Between Us*; *Duke*; *Dash*, winner of the Scott O'Dell Award for Historical Fiction; and *Liberty*. She has also co-written two award-winning picture books: *Two Bobbies: A True Story of Hurricane Katrina, Friendship, and Survival* and *Nubs: The True Story of a Mutt, a Marine & a Miracle*. Kirby lives in Washington State with her husband, Neil, and Winston the Wonder Dog.

When WWII comes to the homefront, these kids and their dogs will have to be brave...

The Dogs of World War II Novels
By Newbery Honor Author Kirby Larson

Meet Audacity Jones—
a heroine with heart!